They Called Her
Mrs. Doc

Janette Oke

They Called Her Mrs. Doc

JO

THEY CALLED HER MRS. DOC
A Bethany House Publication / February 1992
The Janette Oke Collection / 1997

Copyright © 1992 Janette Oke
Reprinted by special arrangement with Bethany House Publishers

Cover by Dan Thornberg, Bethany House staff artist.

Bethany House Publishers
A Ministry of Bethany Fellowship, Inc.
11300 Hampshire Avenue South
Minneapolis, Minnesota 55438

If you would be interested in purchasing additional copies of this book,
please write to this address for information:

The Janette Oke Collection
BDD Direct, Inc.
1540 Broadway
New York, NY 10036

ISBN: 0-553-80579-7

BDD Direct, Inc., 1540 Broadway, New York, New York 10036

Printed in the United States of America

Dedicated with love to
Mrs. Mabelle Oke,
the wonderful mother
of my husband Edward.
Thank you, Mother,
for accepting me as
one of yours
and for sharing your son, and your love,
for the past thirty-five years.

JANETTE OKE was born in Champion, Alberta, during the depression years, to a Canadian prairie farmer and his wife. She is a graduate of Mountain View Bible College in Didsbury, Alberta, where she met her husband, Edward. They were married in May of 1957, and went on to pastor churches in Indiana as well as Calgary and Edmonton, Canada.

The Okes have three sons and one daughter and are enjoying the addition of grandchildren to the family. Edward and Janette have both been active in their local church, serving in various capacities as Sunday school teachers and board members. They make their home in Didsbury, Alberta.

A Tribute

I came into this world one cold February night in a little log farmhouse on the Canadian prairies assisted by Doc Freeze, the same pioneer doctor who delivered most of us in my family as well as many other neighborhood babies. I do not have any firsthand memories of Doc—only memorable and insightful stories. He was almost a legend in the area. Emergency surgeries were performed on kitchen tables with only the light of kerosene lamps for illumination and an ether cloth for anesthetic. His practice stretched for many prairie miles, over rutted or drifted country roads. He worked long hours—any hours—whenever and wherever he was needed.

To him, and to the others like him who served so faithfully and unselfishly in all kinds of weather, under all manner of conditions, I wish to pay tribute. Their devotion to their practice and their people is an inspiration to all.

Contents

Chapter One

Looking Back

She sat on her front porch, the rocker moving so slightly that the gentle swaying was barely detectable. Now and then her hand would lift from the handle of the teacup to swish mechanically at an annoying fly. Strong hands, they were veined and calloused from years of steady tasks, yet delicate even now. Long tapered fingers wrapped securely around the fine china. One hand held the saucer, the other supported the cup, now and then raising the steaming liquid to her lips.

It was a habit of many years, this daily taking of tea on the front porch. She had long since forgotten whether it was the tea or the "belonging" that drew her there, for from her porch rocker she felt as though she had her finger on the pulse of the small community. Her eyes were sharply alive, taking in everything that happened on the street before her.

All around her, life throbbed and echoed. Neighbor called a greeting to neighbor. Mothers chided their little ones for being underfoot. Two elderly gentlemen took the same walk every weekday to pick up the daily paper. Children called and laughed from playgrounds within their fenced yards or clamored for the attention of friends as they ran down the concrete sidewalks to visit the ice cream parlor. She heard their footsteps now against the unyielding surface, and again a slight frown wrinkled her brow. She didn't think she'd ever get used to the concrete. Dull and lifeless, it was just a noise—unlike the board sidewalks of her yesterdays, which had rung with the rhythm of footsteps, seeming to sing and dance beneath the patter of childish feet.

She shifted uneasily and put her cup back on the saucer. There were lots of changes that troubled her—some slightly, others more. It wasn't that she objected to change. She had been thrilled when electricity came to the small town. She had been the first to sign up for the new water and sewer system. And when they bought their first automobile, she was so excited she didn't sleep for three nights.

No, it wasn't change that she objected to, but some changes seemed to take more than they gave. She sighed and sipped her tea again. Like the sidewalks. She had been able to pick out almost every neighbor's footfall when the wooden sidewalks still lined their street. She had known the people's frame of mind by the way they walked. She could have told whether they were out for a pleasant stroll, in a hurry to make a needed purchase before the supper hour, or panicky because of some foreshadowing of calamity.

No, she didn't like all changes. Her rocker moved a bit faster with her agitation. Why couldn't the things that were good—the parts of life that had worked well—just be left alone? Like the sidewalks? Like her own life? She had always been happy—well, no, not always, but mostly, and at least she'd enjoyed some kind of peace. Of course there had been difficult things to face. That was part of living. But along with the trauma had been an underlying sense of tranquility, of stability. She didn't know how one would go about describing it, but she knew it was there. That wonderful sense that no matter what the day might bring, God had things in control.

And that won't change, she consoled herself, and her rocker stopped abruptly with the truth and enormity of the thought.

She shook her head slightly as though to clear her thinking. Of course—of course God wouldn't change. Then why—why did she have this tightness—this nagging pain in the pit of her stomach?

"It will all be so different," she whispered to herself, and in spite of her years of practiced self-discipline a tear gathered in the corner of her eye and trickled down her withered cheek. She did not bother to lift her hand and brush it away, for to do so would have been to admit its presence.

I wish they would just leave me be, she thought again for the hundredth time. "I'm fine here—just fine," she murmured aloud.

But it wasn't to be. She knew that. She also knew that their insistence was because of love and concern.

"But, Mama," she could hear familiar voices saying, "there's no reason for you to stay on here now. We can't care for you here. We worry constantly that something might happen and we wouldn't know until too late."

What could happen? she had wanted to argue.

The worst possible thing in the eyes of her children was that she might die alone. But she was ready for death. She had made her peace with God many years before. She had lived a long eighty-seven years, raised five wonderful children who were now even themselves grandparents. She had shared the long, adventurous life of a wonderful man. She had no inclination to hang on to life.

But of course she didn't argue. She knew her children loved her—worried about her. There had been many times throughout the years when she had worried about them. She understood the concerns of love. So she had simply bargained—bargained for just a little more time.

"Just one more summer in the house," she had begged, her voice taking on a pleading tone that she had never used before with her children. "Just one more summer."

She knew they had chafed at the request. But they had finally kissed her and agreed, adding with an admonishing tone, "You be careful. Get a neighbor boy to do the lawn and for goodness' sake get some man to do your windows. And don't plant so much. There's no one to eat that big garden—and you have far too many flower beds."

It all seemed so reversed—as if she were the child and they the scolding parent.

She'd had her summer—and treasured every minute of

it. But now the chill of fall was in the air. The leaves were beginning to turn and the garden had been harvested, the flower beds put to sleep. She'd been getting almost daily calls. Her new city apartment was waiting. Was she ready for their help with the packing? And that persistent, gnawing little pain was growing ever bigger deep within her. She couldn't put them off much longer. The changes were coming. Big changes, and she dreaded facing them. She just wished she could go on and on—sitting on her familiar front porch, sipping her Red Rose tea, listening to the heartbeat of her own neighborhood. Even the new concrete sidewalk might be a friend—if she could just stay where she was and let life coast to an even and undisturbed stop.

Another tear slid down her cheek. With a steady hand she lifted the cup to her lips again. It was still half full, but now it was cold and unsavory. She set the cup and saucer aside and brushed at her calico apron. She had to get back to her packing. There was so much to do—so much. But she had to do it on her own. How could anyone else possibly know how to sort through her many memories? Yet the new apartment was so limiting in what she could take with her.

A dull thumping came from the concrete and she turned her head to watch two youths running down the street toward her house. She recognized them immediately, as she did all the children of the small town. She found herself wondering if Freddie's fall allergy was giving him the usual trouble, and then she noticed how tall Philip had become.

"One would never have thought it," she whispered, and in spite of her troubled spirit she smiled softly.

Samuel would be so pleased. She thought back to the cold December day when little Philip had first made his appearance.

"How he fought to save that skinny little four-pounder," she murmured to herself. "Never thought he'd make it—but Samuel just wouldn't give up—and look at him now! Bigger than the other fellows his age."

The pounding feet slowed as they reached the front of her house and two pairs of eyes turned toward the porch.

"Hello, Mrs. Doc!" shouted Freddie, and Philip echoed his greeting with a wave of his arm, "Hi, Mrs. Doc."

She responded to their call and then they were running on down the clumping concrete, off on some adventure that only a boy could appreciate.

She smiled after them, thinking of the many times they or other neighborhood children had come to her with a scratch or a sliver or a pet that needed "nursing." She wondered whom they would go to once she was gone.

Mrs. Doc. They all called her that. The whole town seemed to have forgotten her real name was Cassandra Dell Smith, the *wife* of their former doctor. They all seemed to feel as if she belonged to them in some unique and special way. As if she had always belonged to them.

But it hadn't always been so. Her thoughts suddenly dipped back and back, down a lane she had not traveled for many years. She saw again the young girl she had once been—and the many changes that had eventually brought her to where she sat now, on her familiar front porch on a crisp fall day, taking a break from sorting a lifetime of memories.

Chapter Two

A Girl, a Dream

"Cassie Dell Winston—if you don't invite me for this dinner, I'll—I'll never—never speak to you again."

The words were spoken in jest, but Cassie knew instinctively that her longtime friend, Abigail Jordan, was serious about her request. Abigail's dark eyes flashed and her chin set in a stubborn line as she snatched up the cushion from Cassie's vanity bench in mock threat of swinging it at her friend.

Cassie was used to Abigail's overreactions. She lifted her head high, red hair shining and green eyes sparkling in the rays of the afternoon sun. She tipped her head saucily and responded with a slight shrug.

"You always say that," she replied, "but you just go on chattering anyway." She chuckled and turned her back on the threatening cushion.

"Well—well, I'll—I'll never forgive you," blustered Abigail.

Cassie shrugged again. "I've heard that before, too," she answered with another chuckle.

"Well—well—oh—please. Please ask your mother if I might—"

Cassie turned to Abigail and laughed. "I already have and—" she responded and was cut off by a shrill shriek of delight.

16

"You have—oh-h! What did she say? Did she ask my mother? Can I come?"

One question poured out on the heels of another as Abigail threw her arms roughly around her best friend and hugged her. Cassie tugged away from the embrace. "Don't smother me!" she exclaimed in exasperation.

Abigail drew back and squealed again.

"What are we going to wear?" she gasped. "We only have three hours. We—"

"Four," corrected Cassie. "Dinner isn't until seven."

"That still doesn't leave much time. Oh-h." And Abigail groaned.

Cassie tipped her head to one side and observed her agitated friend. "I thought you had no use for doctors," she said with a hint of impatience.

"Well—I—I don't—but they—they aren't doctors—yet. You said so—but they are—they are still young men."

Cassie nodded sagely, took a long look at Abigail, and then giggled. Soon both girls had collapsed on the organdie-covered bed and were laughing with schoolgirl abandon.

Cassandra Dell Winston was the daughter of Dr. Henry P. Winston, noted physician and educator. Not only did he have his own practice in the city of Montreal, but he taught classes of young interns at the local university. Over the years he had handpicked young gentlemen whom he felt were especially promising and invited them home to dinner. It was considered an honor for a young man to be seen as one of Dr. Henry P.'s proteges and almost always promised a shortcut on his way up the ladder of success. Several of Dr. Henry P.'s young men became prominent physicians and surgeons in the city.

Although Cassandra had eyed some of the young men in the past, she had not been of an age where she could be expected to show any serious interest. But this year was different. Cassandra Dell was now seventeen, and though her father would not for a moment have considered her old enough to show interest even yet, her mother knew that somewhere over the last year Cassandra had stepped from childhood to young womanhood.

Being the only girl in the family, Cassie was encouraged to form a close friendship with a girl her own age. Perhaps the Winstons would not have chosen Abigail to be that friend, feeling her to be spoiled, critical, somewhat snooty and immature, but Cassie and Abbie had bonded when the two were starting first grade. They traveled the years together much as sisters—scrapping one minute and inseparable the next.

When they turned twelve, Abbie had announced to the world that from now on she would answer only to *Abigail,* and she did, too. Cassie thought she was making too much of it, but she complied also.

But some things about Abigail irked even Cassie. One was the way she put on airs about her father's profession. He was a well-known attorney, and Abigail was always making little comments about her father's prestige in the city, the cost of her silks and satins, the maid who looked after her boudoir.

Cassie's father was not poor. They lived in one of the best sections of the city—just down the street from Abigail herself. It was true that Abigail's house was bigger. It was also true that they had two more household staff than did the Winstons, and it was true that her closets bulged with dresses that she hardly ever wore. But Cassie did not feel like the poor country cousin, and she resented it when Abigail made her snippy little remarks.

Still, they were best of friends, even when the one piqued the other. Now with the coming dinner, Abigail was almost fawning. Impatient again, Cassie turned her back, her chin coming up, and for a moment she wished she hadn't coaxed an invitation out of her mother.

"There are two of them?" Abigail was asking, giving Cassie's arm a little tug.

"Three," responded Cassie with a casual flip of her red curls. "Three."

"Oh," squealed Abigail. "Just think. Three." Shaking Cassie's arm again, she hurried another question. "Do you know their names?" she probed.

Cassie faced Abigail, her head cocked slightly to the right. "Oh yes. Father has us practicing the names long before they arrive."

She turned to the mirror and brushed at an annoying freckle on her left cheek.

"Well, tell me the names," demanded Abigail. "I need to practice, too."

Cassie looked full at her friend. Excitement had colored the girl's cheeks and caused her dark eyes to flash. She was really quite attractive. Cassie wondered if she had done the right thing in inviting another girl to share the dinner table. What if Abigail stole the show? What if one of the young gentlemen looked—well, suitable—and then he choose Abigail instead of her? Cassie trembled at the thought and then shook off the fear along with Abigail's restricting hand.

"The oldest one is Dr. Corouthers. He has already graduated and is just beginning his internship."

"Is he really *old*?" asked Abigail with a grimace, then added quickly, "You may have him."

Cassie flipped back a straying lock of hair and gave her friend a disdainful look. Abigail did not even cringe.

"Then there is Mr. Birdwell—"

"Birdwell! What an awful name. I would never—never allow myself to become Abigail Birdwell. That's awful. Horrible!"

Cassie reached up to draw the pins from her hair and let it spill about her shoulders. She shook her head in impatience and turned those flashing green eyes on her friend. "You do not have to stay for dinner," she reminded the girl coolly. "And you certainly do not have to become Mrs. Abigail Birdwell."

She sat down in front of the vanity mirror and noticed the angry flush in her face.

"Well, after all," Abigail responded, seeing no need to apologize, "it is all in good fun. What is the name of the third one?"

"Mr. Smith," said Cassie.

"Mr. Smith? You're teasing me, aren't you?"

"No, I am not."

"Really? It's really just—just Mr. Smith?"

Cassie let her fingers gently trace another freckle. "I assume he has a given name," she said tartly.

"Well, I do hope Walton or Jefferson or—or—"

"Oh, do stop carrying on so," Cassie responded, annoyance edging her voice, "or I'll wish I had never invited you."

A pout began to pucker Abigail's mouth. "Sometimes you can be most old-maidish," she said. To which Cassie replied with a clipped, "And sometimes you can be most childish."

Heavy silence invaded the room. Cassie continued to study her face in the mirror and Abigail moved restlessly on the organdie coverlet.

"Would you rather I didn't come?" she asked peevishly at length, her words daring Cassie to refuse her admittance.

"Oh, let's not fight," Cassie replied, turning to her almost reluctantly. "I told Mama that I don't wish to be the only girl at a whole table full of men and boys. She's already asked your mother, and you've been given permission. So why don't you run on home and get ready. Be back here by seven—sharp. Mama hates for anyone to be late."

"You're a dear!" exclaimed Abigail and bounced up to give Cassie a quick hug. "I will be here by seven—in my prettiest silk and my emerald choker."

Yes, thought Cassie, turning back to her mirror, *I'm sure you will—even though you think yourself way above any of the three young men.* She knew Abigail, the "unattainable attorney's daughter," would still try her hardest to impress them.

Her shoulder sagged slightly as she heard her bedroom door open and close and Abigail's light footsteps hurrying down the carpeted hall.

Cassie was certain now that she should never have invited Abigail to join the dinner party. Abigail's dark brown eyes and almost raven black hair made a striking contrast with her creamy skin, and she had no freckles whatever. It was true that her nose was a tad long, her chin had a stubborn tilt, and her manners sometimes left things to be desired, but Cassie still felt a twinge of fear that it might be Abigail who would steal the show.

"Oh, bother!" she said disgustedly. "Why didn't I just let well enough alone?"

Then she shrugged again. "They most likely will all be old—and boring—and—and ugly," she consoled her image in the mirror. "Abigail is right—doctors aren't really very good catches. Just look at Papa. He's always busy—never home—and terribly old-fashioned."

She heaved a sigh and rose from the vanity stool. She still hadn't decided what she would wear—but for some reason it no longer seemed so terribly important.

———

The ten people at the dinner table included Dr. and Mrs. Henry P. Winston, the three gentlemen dinner guests, Cassie and Abigail and Cassie's three younger brothers.

Cassie tried to be ladylike in manner and decorum, but it was difficult at times with Abigail surreptitiously kicking her under the table and giving her sly glances and knowing nods. Cassie was about to lose patience again when Abigail seemed to stop her twittering and settle down, content to catch shy peeks from behind long, dark lashes at the three distinguished dinner guests.

Cassie's own head was still spinning. The "older" Dr. Corouthers had turned out to not be so old after all. In fact, he didn't look a bit over twenty-six or seven. Still quite acceptable in Cassie's thinking. And the younger Mr. Birdwell did not at all resemble his name. He was quite striking with a mass of wavy blond hair and the bluest eyes she had ever seen.

Mr. Smith was the quietest of the lot, seeming to speak only when spoken to. He was as plain as his name, in Cassie's estimation—but he did have a gentle, pleasant smile and first-class manners. Cassie watched her mother chatting quite easily with him at one end of the table, while Dr. Henry

P. discussed medical topics with the other two dinner guests and kept his three young sons in order with frequent stern looks.

For the most part, Cassie and Abigail seemed to go unnoticed. Cassie could not help but wonder if Abigail chafed that her beautiful creamy silk and the expensive emerald choker were ignored. As the thought crossed Cassie's mind, she was tempted to savor her friend's discomfiture, but quickly brought herself in check when she remembered that she, too, had been as casually overlooked. She felt her cheeks flush slightly and for one awful moment had the urge to do something outlandish just to get some attention.

Her breeding stood her in good stead. Quietly and with the best of manners she continued the meal, only occasionally stealing an upward glance at the three opposite dinner guests.

The meal was almost over and the three were making elaborate compliments to Mrs. Winston when Cassie felt eyes upon her and cast a quick glance in the direction of Mr. Birdwell, hoping to find him solemnly studying her great beauty. But Mr. Birdwell had his eyes fastened on the rosy face of Abigail. Cassie looked away quickly.

"You have only the one daughter, Mrs. Winston?" she heard a deep but soft voice inquire, and her head almost jerked up.

"One girl," responded Mrs. Winston. "One girl and three boys."

Cassie carefully turned her head.

"It's rather a shame," the same voice continued. "I'm sure the neighborhood young men wish that you had provided at least a dozen."

Cassie could not have controlled it. She found herself looking into a pair of teasing but kind eyes. Her face reddened as she quickly dropped her gaze from Mr. Smith's and listened to her mother reply calmly, "Our Cassie is quickly becoming an attractive young woman. I am sure that Dr. Winston will soon need to guard the front door." Her mother's soft laughter followed the statement. Cassie had never heard her speak in such a fashion before and it confused and troubled her. She wished she could escape the table—and the eyes of Mr. Smith—to the safety of her own room.

Then she lifted her chin slightly and her red head gave a bit of a nod. If they were having fun at her expense, she would spoil it for them by not responding. She looked directly across the table at Mr. Corouthers and tipped her head slightly. "And are you from our area, Dr. Corouthers?" Her smile was confident.

Cassie felt more than heard the quick intake of Abigail's breath.

But Dr. Corouthers seemed pleased to be questioned. "I'm from Halifax," he answered evenly. "Have you been there?"

Cassie was "committed" now, and she wished with all her trembling heart that she had not been so bold. But she paused only a moment and continued. "Only once. Papa had a conference there and we all went with him when I was— was—" She had been about to say "when I was twelve." Instead, she finished lamely, "When I was younger."

"And did you like it?" asked Mr. Corouthers with interest.

Cassie nodded, a smile lighting her face in spite of herself. "I especially liked the tall ships," she admitted, but didn't bother to add that at the time she had been quite put out with the fact that she was born a girl rather than a boy. She had thought she would love to be a sailor.

"Cassie thinks she'd like to sail," put in younger brother Paul, and Cassie wished she could have withered him with a look.

"I've always wanted to sail, too," replied Dr. Corouthers, nodding companionably. "I have not given up the dream."

"Have you manned a boat?" questioned Mr. Birdwell, entering the conversation.

"We always had a skiff—but it wasn't what one would put out to sea in. I've always dreamed of having a real craft— one that would challenge the open waters."

"We had a little boat once," offered Mr. Birdwell. "Just a rickety little piece of flimsy boards—hardly more than a crate—but we spent hours on the local pond. She sank on me

24

once and I found myself in up to my chin. I hadn't learned to swim at the time, but my father soon saw to it that I'd at least be able to make my way ashore if it happened again. . . ."

Cassie bowed out of the discussion as others around the table joined in the conversation.

Well, at least they know I'm here, she thought with some satisfaction. *Actually, I'm the one who introduced a more spirited topic than Papa's continuing classroom lecture.*

And for that one brief moment of glory, Cassie was gratified. She had entered the conversation, been accepted, and had not been challenged in the least by her parents for having done so.

Chapter Three

Girl Talk

"Isn't he wonderful?" Abigail enthused, throwing herself on the chintz window seat. The dinner had ended, the men retiring to the library to discuss medical discoveries, and the girls to Cassie's bedroom.

Cassie joined her on the window seat but did not answer. She wasn't quite sure what she was supposed to say or whom Abigail was so excited about.

"Did you see the way he looked at me?" Abigail continued to marvel.

Cassie was still thinking of her brief but captivating exchange with Dr. Corouthers. Perhaps in the future she would even dare to speak with Mr. Birdwell. He was so nice looking—had such attractive blue eyes.

"I am sure he likes me," Abigail rambled on. "I could see it in his eyes. Did you notice? Did you see—?"

"No," said Cassie, looking rather forthrightly at her twittering friend. "No. I didn't see it."

"Birdwell," Abigail rushed on without a pause. She tipped her head slightly to one side. "It isn't a pleasing name at all—but the gentleman wears it well."

"You think that Mr. Birdwell has fallen for you?" Cassie asked Abigail directly.

"Didn't you see him? He looked right at me. I—I just could have died!" She laughed self-consciously and added, "I was sure I'd spill my tea or drop my fried chicken in my lap or something. I was so—so—nervous." When Cassie said nothing, Abigail too fell silent.

Cassie was willing to admit that Mr. Birdwell was a fine-looking young man. Her thoughts went even further. She fervently hoped that he did not find Abigail too attractive. There would be more dinner parties, many evening meetings, perhaps even a Saturday outing with the young gentlemen. There always were when her father took young doctors under his personal tutorage. Cassie was bound to see the young man again. All three of the young men. She would have ample time to decide if she preferred Dr. Corouthers or Mr. Birdwell. But she wanted to be able to make the choice. She did not wish her options limited by the interference of Abigail.

"Did your mother say that they are coming to dinner again next week?" Abigail broke the silence.

Cassie lifted her head and nodded slowly. She could not deny it. But she did wonder how she would gently ease her lifetime friend out of the picture.

"I thought you didn't like doctors," she reminded the girl.

"Well," observed Abigail nonchalantly, "maybe he will change his mind about being one—maybe he won't even be a doctor if he finds that I prefer attorneys."

"I suppose you'll have him change his name as well." Cassie winced inwardly at her own flippant remark, but Abigail didn't even notice.

"Oh, do you really think he would? I'm sure Papa would do all the legal work free of charge. We could pick something our very own. Something romantic—something—"

"Oh, Abigail," said Cassie, standing abruptly to her feet and tossing a pillow carelessly at the other young woman.

Abigail looked up in surprise. "What's wrong with you?" she demanded.

"You," Cassie shot back. "If he isn't good enough the way he is, then why don't you just forget about him? 'Change his name.' 'Change his occupation.' Why don't you have him change the color of his eyes?"

"Oh no," Abigail responded innocently. "I love his eyes."

Cassie threw another pillow. But Abigail caught it and drew it close. She sighed a long, contented sigh and murmured dreamily, "I can hardly wait to see him again."

"And when do you expect that to be?" questioned Cassie, shutting her window with a loud bang.

"Next week," replied Abigail.

"You think Mama is going to invite you for dinner every time we have guests?"

"Oh, Cassie, please. Please! You just *have* to get me another invitation. You are still the only girl. Remember. 'The only girl in a room full of men and boys.' "

Cassie cocked her head in pretended thought. "That might not be so bad," she observed.

"Oh, you're not serious! You wouldn't possibly leave me out. I mean, we have been friends—best friends—for years. You couldn't possibly turn on me now. Could you?"

"Do you invite me to your house when your parents have young attorneys in for dinner?" asked Cassie frankly.

"We never have young attorneys—you know that. Papa said that he had to make it on his own. He sees no sense in coddling the competition. Give them a couple years and they will be fighting him in court."

"It's not that way with doctors," said Cassie thoughtfully. "Doctors help one another all they can. They are not 'competition.' They are—are partners. The world needs all the doctors we can produce, Papa says. Good doctors. He feels very strongly about it."

"Well, your papa and my papa see things differently," admitted Abigail.

"Yes. Yes," mused Cassie. "They certainly do." And for some reason she couldn't explain, Cassie suddenly felt a surge of pride for her papa.

"Dr. Henry P. Winston," she said aloud. "You know, there are many people who have a good deal of respect for that name."

Abigail looked at her as though Cassie was losing her mind. Then she shrugged her shoulders and moved toward the door.

"I have to get home. Papa said for me to call Wilbur to come and walk me. May I use the phone in the front hall?"

"Of course," nodded Cassie and followed her out to walk her friend down to the entrance hall. Wilbur was Abigail's older brother. Cassie had never been fond of the boy. He was much too arrogant and pompous to make a good friend for anyone.

"You will get me another invitation, won't you?" Abigail pleaded as they descended the stairs together.

"I'll see" was all that Cassie would promise.

They stopped in the hall while Abigail made her call. From the study came the sound of voices. The four men seemed to be deep in discussion.

". . . I still think research should be able to isolate the germ," said a voice that Cassie thought to be Mr. Smith's.

"I agree," her father joined in. "If only we had funds and equipment and someone with the desire to see the project—"

Abigail completed her call and the two girls moved down the hall and out of earshot.

"I'll wait outside with you until Wilbur comes," offered Cassie.

The evening was pleasant and the minutes passed quickly. Soon Wilbur's heavy steps announced his approach. Cassie drew back into the shadows. She was in no mood to take Wilbur's teasing about her carrot-top, her green cat eyes, or her freckles.

"I'll see you tomorrow," she whispered to Abigail and disappeared up the walk before Wilbur could even call after her.

———

Over the winter months the young men did come again. Abigail was not always invited to be Cassie's guest, but she did come often enough to feel that she was making significant headway with the attractive Mr. Birdwell. She had even discovered that his first name was Mitchell.

"Mitchell is a nice name," she had whispered one evening to Cassie as they had left the table and retired to her room to share newly garnered information. "Do you suppose he might be talked into using it as a last? Abigail Mitchell. That would sound just fine."

Cassie gave her friend a withering look and wondered about Dr. Corouthers' first name. She didn't dare ask and her papa never referred to the young men by their given names.

"Did you hear what Mitchell called Mr. Smith?" went on Abigail.

Cassie shook her head.

"Sam! Sam? Can you imagine anything more—more *drab*. Sam Smith. Chopped off and—and ugly. As ugly as the man himself."

"That's not fair," Cassie heard herself responding. "He's not ugly."

"Well, he certainly isn't handsome."

"There's a lot of room between handsome and ugly," retorted Cassie, surprising herself by sticking up for the young man. She really had paid very little attention to him at all. But he did have a winsome smile, and her mama thought him terribly mannerly, and her papa, for reasons of his own, seemed to think that the young Mr. Smith was going to make a wonderful doctor someday. In fact, Cassie heard him talking about Smith even more than about Birdwell or Corouthers.

"Papa says he will be a good doctor," went on Cassie. "He has very high regard for him."

"But he's so uncommonly plain," continued Abigail mournfully. "And—and he looks so boyish with that bit of hair falling over his forehead as it does. You'd think that a *doctor* would try to get it under proper control. Wet it down or slick it back or—"

"One should not be judged on appearance alone," cut in Cassie, repeating words she had heard from her father and had detested hearing up to that point.

Abigail stopped mid-stride. "Do you *like* him or something?" she queried.

"Of course. I mean—I—I have no reason not to like him. Oh, I don't like him like—" She had been about to say "like

Mitchell Birdwell," but checked herself in time. "I—I like all three of the young men that Papa has picked. I—I just don't swoon over them like you do, that's all."

"Well, I don't swoon over them either," insisted Abigail. "At least not over all of them. Just—just Mitchell, and I'm sure it isn't all on my side either. Did you see how he smiled at me at the table? I'm sure he is just waiting for the proper time to ask to call."

Cassie was no longer prepared to deny Abigail's charge. She had smiled at the young Mr. Birdwell herself on a few occasions, but there wasn't much response—so it seemed. She had decided to turn her attention elsewhere and concentrate on Dr. Corouthers instead.

By carefully playing detective, she learned that his name was Taylor Corouthers. He was twenty-nine. More than eleven years her senior. She had no problem envisioning herself with an older, mature, stable man. Her own papa was nine years her mama's senior. What did bother her was that Dr. Corouthers always spoke of returning to Halifax at the end of his internship. Cassie had no intention of leaving her Montreal home and journeying to a land that was not nearly as cultured or refined as she considered her home city to be—even if it did have ships!

"I'll just have to persuade him to stay on here," she told herself. "Papa will be able to find him a good position, a practice right in Montreal."

And Cassie put this concern from her head and concentrated on looking her best and acting her most charming. She was sure Dr. Corouthers had indeed noticed her; and with her eighteenth birthday fast approaching, she was prepared to be courted in proper fashion.

For the first time in many years, Cassie did not share her inner thoughts with Abigail. They seemed too personal, too special, perhaps too fragile to be shared, even with her best friend.

———

Cassie was home alone when the doorbell rang. Dickerson, the butler, answered and came to the drawing room where Cassie was reading before the fire.

"Mr. Smith is waiting in the hall," he said with his usual formal manner.

"But Papa is out. He and Mama have taken the boys to the ball game."

"Yes, Miss. I know the evening's plans," Dickerson said stiffly. "But the fact remains, Mr. Smith is waiting in the front hall. He says that he will speak with you in the absence of your father."

Cassie rose reluctantly from her comfortable chair, brushing at her skirt to whisk away any wrinkles.

"Well," she informed Dickerson, "show him in."

An eyebrow raised. "In here, Miss?"

"Why not?" she retorted somewhat shortly. "You said he wishes to see me in place of my father. Then show him in."

"Very well, Miss," replied Dickerson curtly, but Cassie knew that the elderly butler did not think it was "very well" at all.

She laid her book on the small table and turned to face the door. Soon footsteps approached and Mr. Smith stood before her, his gentle smile crinkling the corners of his eyes and lighting his face with good humor. "I am dreadfully sorry to be disturbing you, Miss Winston," he began, "but I have some papers for your father and have a bit of explanation to go with them."

"I expect my father to be back very soon," Cassie was quick to assure him. "Rather than try to explain things to me, perhaps you would have a cup of tea—or coffee—and await his return."

"Oh, but I wouldn't intrude—"

"No intrusion. I have been reading. The story will wait. Have a seat here by the fire. It isn't really cold but the evenings can hold a bit of a chill."

Then Cassie turned to the shocked Dickerson. "Would you see that we are served, please?" she said quietly. "I believe that Mr. Smith prefers coffee to tea." Dickerson left without a word.

Samuel Smith's eyebrows shot up as he studied her, and then a smile twitched his lips, suggesting that perhaps she was not the child he had taken her to be.

"Now, be seated, please," she invited, waving one slender hand at the chairs before the fire.

"Thank you," Mr. Smith responded, his voice edged with humor at the turn of events.

"So you do not care for football?" he asked as he lowered himself into the overstuffed chair and held his hands toward the blaze in the fireplace.

"As my parents' only daughter—I decided to be just that," Cassie responded good-naturedly. "They have enough company taking my three brothers."

"But your mother enjoys the game?"

Cassie had never stopped to wonder about that fact before.

"I guess she does," she responded slowly. "I really don't know why. At first I think that she felt Papa needed help with three energetic young boys. Then—well—then I guess she maybe grew to like it."

He chuckled softly. Cassie liked his laugh.

"Wouldn't you possibly learn to like it?"

She cocked her head to one side and thought about his query. "Perhaps," she responded, "but I really see no need to put myself out to try. I'm—I'm rather a book-and-fireside person. I much prefer the warmth here to the chill of the wind out there."

A silence threatened to become awkward. "And you?" asked Cassie quickly.

"I love the sport. I only wish that I had time to go. Although, I must admit that I'd rather be playing than sitting in the stands."

Cassie looked at him with new eyes. Yes, he likely would enjoy sports. He was of medium height, with a rather broad build and appeared to be solid. She nodded her head and made no reply.

"What are you reading?" he surprised her by asking.

She reached for her book and turned it so he could see the cover. "It's *Wuthering Heights*," she admitted a bit apologetically. "I—I read it fairly regularly."

"And your fancy goes to Heathcliff?" he prompted.

Cassie felt her face flushing. She was glad that Dickerson arrived with the coffee tray before she had to answer.

The conversation flowed on over their steaming cups. Cassie had never entertained a young gentleman before and was surprised how easy he made her task. In fact, it really wasn't that much more difficult than chatting with Abigail.

As the minutes passed by in conversation, she discovered many little bits of personal information about her guest, but she eventually realized he had gently probed to find out even more about her.

By the time the back door slammed, announcing the return of her parents and brothers from the game, Cassie felt she had made a friend. She was almost sorry to have their evening end.

She rose, and he stood with her. "If you'll excuse me," she said, "I'll tell my father that you are waiting to see him."

"Thank you," he replied sincerely. "Thank you—for the coffee—the conversation—and the delightful company."

She blushed slightly and moved toward the sound of excited voices.

"We won!" she heard young Simon informing Cook. "We won. Just trounced 'em good."

But Cassie hardly noticed. Instead, her thoughts were on the young man in the parlor. He did have a very pleasant smile. And she found that lock of undisciplined hair rather—rather appealing.

Chapter Four

Preparations

Cassie stretched lazily, and wiggled her head on the thick downy pillow to find the most comfortable position. Her bright hair spilled out around her and she picked up a strand and studied it as though seeing it for the first time.

"It sure is red," she muttered under her breath.

She had never liked her red hair. It always drew attention until she felt as if she were some kind of circus sideshow.

"It might as well be lime green—or royal blue with all the stares I get," she mumbled further and whipped the tresses aside. "Red hair and freckles! They are a curse from God."

As soon as Cassie had murmured the words she was instantly contrite. Her mother had always told her that God knew best in His choosing and that the bright red hair set her apart from other young girls her own age.

But Cassie was not at an age to enjoy being set apart. She wanted to be attractive—yes—but not *different*.

If I could choose—could choose to look any way I wanted— what would I pick? wondered Cassie.

A smile played about her lips as she played her little game.

"I would have creamy, unfreckled skin," she murmured dreamily. At least that part was very easy. "Then I would have—blond hair—just as blond as hair can be. Like—like corn silk—or—maybe that's too yellowy. Or dark hair. That would show my skin off more. With—with deep blue eyes I think—or chocolaty brown—they look—"

A knock on her door interrupted her monologue. She looked toward the door, judged the intrusion to be Nettie, the maid, flipped over on her side and feigned sleep.

She heard the door open.

"Cassie. Cassie, it's past nine." It was her mother's voice. "You really need to develop better rising habits. One cannot spend one's time loafing about in bed."

Mrs. Winston crossed the carpeted floor and raised the window shade. Bright sun streamed into the room.

Cassie moved and stretched and pretended to be awakened from a deep sleep, but her mother did not seem to be fooled for one minute.

"I've arranged with Cook for some kitchen lessons," she continued. "But if you don't soon get to the kitchen, she'll need to begin preparing lunch."

"Cooking lessons?" said Cassie in disbelief.

"Yes, cooking. You are no longer a child. We have put it off long enough. You must learn how to find your way around the kitchen."

"But—"

"No arguments. A girl your age should have learned long ago."

"Whatever for?" asked Cassie candidly.

"So you will know how to properly prepare a meal," went on Mrs. Winston. "Here you are almost eighteen and you know nothing more than making sugar cookies and icing a cake."

Cassie's feet hit the floor at the same time her red-haired temper flared.

"Are you saying that I am destined to be a cook?"

"Certainly not," replied her mother, unruffled by Cassie's outspokenness. "I am saying that a girl who is nearing marriageable age should know how to prepare something more than cookies for her household."

"That's a cook's job," insisted Cassie.

"That's a wife's job," responded Mrs. Winston.

"You don't cook," Cassie flung at her, drawing a gingham dress from her wardrobe and preparing to head for the bathroom.

"I don't—but I could," Mrs. Winston said calmly. "If anything should happen to Cook, the family would still have meals."

Cassie had never seen her mother in the kitchen, so she cast a disdainful glance her way and moved to pick clean lingerie from a dresser drawer.

"I will expect you in the kitchen, prepared—body and mind—in twenty minutes," Mrs. Winston said firmly and she left the room, closing the door behind her.

Cassie was not in a good mood as she went to draw her bath. In the first place, her little fantasy game had been interrupted. Secondly, she was in no mind to scrub carrots and peel potatoes. That was Cook's job. And she certainly had no intention of handling uncooked meat. She hated it. Hated the smell. Hated the sight of the oozing blood. Hated the fact that it had once been a part of something living and moving. She shuddered at the very thought and turned the water on with more force.

But as Cassie stretched herself out in the warm water, her thoughts did an about-turn.

What was her mother saying? Why had she suddenly taken it upon herself to arrange for cooking lessons? Why had her mother spoken of her being near marriageable age? Did she really feel that Cassie was growing up—that a young man might soon come calling?

Certainly Cassie had been entertaining those thoughts— but her *mother*?

Cassie felt a tingle go all through her body, and instead of her usual languishing in the tub, dawdling her way through her dressing and the pinning of her hair, excitement hurried her out and into her clothes.

She was in the kitchen well within the twenty minutes, prepared both in body and mind for the cooking lesson.

Cook began her morning's instruction with the making of bread. At first it was exciting, but Cassie soon discovered it was a slow and tedious task, and one had to wait for such a long, long time for the bread to rise. Cassie begged to be excused while the process went on and Cook agreed, saying she needed her kitchen for preparing the noon meal. Cassie should be back in the kitchen at two o'clock.

Cassie was glad to slip out the back door to the gardens. She hoped to hide behind the ivy vines in the gazebo and continue her "daydreaming."

But her mother was seated in the shade on the porch swing, a piece of handwork occupying her fingers. She was always embroidering or hemming or stitching this or that. Cassie had often wondered what intrigued her mother about needlework, but she had never thought to ask.

"Is the bread set?" asked Mrs. Winston.

Cassie nodded and went to ease her way past the swing.

"I have something for you," said Mrs. Winston, patting the seat beside her, and Cassie had no choice but to join her mother.

Cassie's brow puckered slightly as her mother handed her a bit of stitchery. It seemed that her mother was intent on remedying Cassie's neglect in household training all in one fell swoop.

Cassie sighed and picked up the piece of material. A needle was stuck in with a long white thread trailing out behind it. As bidden, she turned her eyes reluctantly toward her mother's hands to watch the movements of a skilled seamstress. It didn't look difficult and Cassie plunged ahead, but she was soon to discover that her own stitches certainly did not compare with those of her mother's.

"You hurry too much," her mother admonished. "One must be slow and accurate. The speed will come as you practice."

Cassie tried again, biting her lip in concentration as she slipped the needle in and out of the cloth. Although she wore the provided thimble, she managed to prick her finger and had to stop for a few moments so she wouldn't get drops of blood on the piece.

But her mother would not excuse her. They stitched on

until the signal was given for the noon meal. Cassie was so glad to hear the chime.

But on the way to the luncheon table her mother said firmly, "You may rest for an hour after lunch. You can check with Cook on how the bread is coming—then join me again on the porch. Actually, you are doing quite well with your sampler."

Cassie's mouth began to droop in a pout.

"That is very unbecoming for a young lady," her mother surprised her by stating. "When one becomes a man, one is to put away childish things—and the same holds true for a woman."

Cassie's head lifted in frustration and defiance. Of course, she wanted to be a young woman—be treated like a lady— but surely it didn't mean that you ceased being yourself and had to be someone totally different. Totally remade. That was unfair of the adult world. For a moment she wished to stamp her slippered foot, but one look into her mother's serious eyes and she changed her mind and swished her skirts instead. Cassie knew from experience that her mother seldom acted as the disciplinarian of the family—but when she did, she wasn't to be crossed.

For one brief, silent moment the two strong wills clashed, and then Mrs. Winston moved forward to lead the way to the dining room.

"It is your choice," she said in a half whisper, for the three boys, faces scrubbed and hair slicked back, were coming within earshot. "Your choice whether you wish to be a child or an adult. No one can manage both."

Then Mrs. Winston turned to her sons, smiled as though nothing out of the ordinary was going on and patted Stephen on the shoulder. She asked them how they had been spending their day, and each one clamored to be first in the telling. Her indulgent smile seemed to say, "When I was a child, I spoke as a child. . . ."

But Cassie hardly noticed. She could not shift her thoughts so easily or quickly. Her sour mood continued. Life did not seem at all fair. It had been good to her thus far. She had been raised in a home where there were more than ample material blessings—they were plentiful. She had been gently nurtured, trained in all of the finer graces. She had been pampered and petted and her fancies had been humored. She played or loafed or dreamed at her own whims. And now, suddenly, just because her mother deemed that she was soon to be courted, she was asked to leave behind her enjoyable times and devote her hours to tedious kitchen chores and plying a needle endlessly in and out of boring material. Who made the rules for adulthood, anyway? And why did they insist that nothing be fun anymore?

Cassie's thoughts went further. In her own thinking she was certainly prepared for courting. It would be most exciting to have a young man pay homage—bringing flowers and chocolates and spending his time thinking of nice little pleasantries to say to make her cheeks glow with a blush, or spend his hours dreaming and counting the minutes until he would see her face again. But Cassie's thoughts had gone no further than the courting. The fun and excitement. She had not thought of marriage—or the duties of marriage. Now she wasn't sure that marriage was altogether desirable. Wasn't it rather—rather permanent—and boring? Oh, she knew that Abigail spoke of marriage—at least to the changing of her name. But she wasn't sure that Abigail was really ready for all of the duties of marriage either. The privileges maybe—but not the responsibilities. Cassie could not envision Abigail in the kitchen, an ample apron wrapped around her small frame, flour on her nose as she kneaded bread dough. Nor could she picture Abigail seated on a porch swing, dutifully plying her needle in and out of a swatch of linen. That wasn't what she and Abigail had had in mind when they had set their minds on being courted.

Cassie stirred restlessly in her chair. She wasn't sure her mother understood what it was like to be a young lady.

———

That evening Cassie was glad to see Abigail drop in for a visit. She wanted to have someone with whom to discuss the terrifying changes that were taking place in her world.

"And Mother has suddenly decided that I must know all the duties of a grown-up. Even cooking and—"

"You are learning to *cook*?" squealed Abigail.

"Bread! Today I had a lesson in baking bread. Can you imagine? When will I ever need to know how to bake bread?" Cassie groaned.

"I'd love to cook!" cried Abigail in ecstasy. "I've coaxed and coaxed Mother—but she insists that I would drive Cook mad if I were allowed in the kitchen."

Cassie could only stare at her friend as though she had taken leave of her senses.

"Whatever for?" she asked incredulously.

"I think it would be fun. I've always wanted to make things. Not for—for a duty, of course. But just for the fun."

"But it's not fun," insisted Cassie. "It's dreadfully boring. Do you have any idea how long it takes bread to decide to rise? Hours and hours. And you just have to wait on it. Of course, Cook usually mixes it up first thing in the morning— even before breakfast, and then she has it over and done with early in the day. I was until five o'clock getting the last loaf from the oven." She groaned again.

"Did it taste good?" asked Abigail.

Cassie threw her a disdainful look. "How would I know? I never tasted it."

Abigail seemed to know better than to question why.

"And I burned my finger," went on Cassie, studying the blister on her first finger. "In one day—a burn and a prick. In just one day."

Abigail giggled.

"It's not funny," Cassie shot back in irritation. "You—you just wait until your mother takes a notion—"

"My mother won't. She doesn't even know how to do any of those things herself." Abigail sighed a long sigh that sounded almost mournful to Cassie.

They sat in silence for a few moments, mulling over the

fact that their thinking was suddenly going in opposite directions. It was a surprise to each of them.

"Do you think—," Abigail ventured at last, "that your mother might let me—you know—sort of be with you in the kitchen?"

Cassie could not have been more shocked.

"You want to learn how to cook?"

"Just for fun. Not that I'll ever need to do it or anything. But just for fun."

Cassie pondered the question. "I think that Cook feels I am more than enough to deal with. She seemed awfully pleased to get rid of me today," admitted Cassie.

"Maybe I could help," said Abigail brightly.

Cassie shook her head. Things had gone from bad to worse. "I don't know," she said hesitantly. "I doubt that Mother will agree—but I guess I could ask."

Abigail rewarded her with another squeal and a quick hug.

Chapter Five

Rites of Passage

Over the weeks that followed, Cassie grudgingly began to fall into her mother's routine. There were kitchen lessons, sewing assignments, and even household chores, considered to be her "training" for days ahead. She still fussed about the duties and on occasion spoke her mind, but her agitation gradually lessened. Her mother smiled approvingly at each small sign of progress.

The dinners with her father's students now included one more young man.

"I'm afraid Abigail can no longer be a dinner guest," Mrs. Winston informed Cassie. "It just doesn't work for the table seating."

"The table can easily hold an even dozen," Cassie reminded her, but Mrs. Winston turned a deaf ear.

"Besides," she continued, "when the two of you are together, neither of you act your age."

Cassie turned flashing eyes on her mother, but Mrs. Winston had already moved toward the kitchen to give further orders to Cook.

Cassie wheeled from the room, her skirts swishing angrily. It was unfair for her mother to make such a charge. Even after her own moments of pique about sharing the attention, she would miss Abigail. Who would there be to share little nudges or upraised eyebrows? The grown-ups could be so stuffy and her brothers so childish. No one else at table ever seemed to be of like mind with her.

Then Cassie's cheeks began to flame. That was exactly what her mother had been talking about. She and Abigail did indeed keep sending silent messages to each other. Perhaps they were a bit silly. Cassie's chin came up and she determined to be a part of the adult conversation around the table—not just one of the children.

The change in the dinner arrangements was not received lightly by Abigail.

"Why?" she moaned and stewed. "Why am I just—put out?"

"You aren't put out," Cassie argued.

"But what about Mr. Birdwell? I am sure he was about to ask if he could call."

"He can still call. He knows very well that you are just a few houses down the street."

"But Papa would never entertain a mere doctor," went on Abigail.

"A mere doctor has been feeding you as often as your own father has," Cassandra reminded Abigail. Her cheeks burned and she swung on her heel and began fluffing the pillows on her bed.

"I'm sorry. I didn't mean it that way," Abigail had the grace to apologize. "It's just that Papa—well he is rather—rather restrictive in his views. He—he still sees me as a child. And I'll be eighteen next month. I'm sure I'm destined to be an old maid."

In spite of herself, Cassie felt sorry for Abigail. Her temper began to cool and she stopped thumping pillows and turned back to her friend.

"With your looks?" she exclaimed. "Impossible!"

The remark seemed to comfort Abigail. She reached up to tuck a wayward curl back into a side comb. "Do you think that Mr. Birdwell might ask to call?"

Cassie secretly felt that Abigail had been flirting shamelessly with the young man for many weeks and was tempted to speak her mind, but instead she answered demurely, "I shouldn't be surprised."

Abigail, pleased, said, "Remind him that I am absent by no choice of my own." She paused and went on. "And you might also point out my house again."

Cassie nodded—but she was no longer in the mood to placate Abigail. She turned to her vanity and began to undo her hair so she might pin it properly for the evening's dinner. Suddenly she felt a jerk on her arm.

"Did you say that your father is bringing another young gentleman?" Abigail demanded.

Cassie pulled her arm away from Abigail's grip. "You heard me," she said with a bit of annoyance. "That is why there isn't room for you at the table."

"Another one! I wonder what he will be like. Do you know his name? Is he good-looking?"

Cassie turned back to her hair. She had not realized how fickle and childish her lifelong friend was. "What happened to Mr. Birdwell? Remember him?"

Abigail reached down and picked up one of Cassie's silver side combs. "Well—it's not as though he has come calling yet or anything," she reasoned.

"No. No, he hasn't been calling," agreed Cassie. In fact, neither of the girls had enjoyed a formal caller, and Cassie herself remembered that she too had an eighteenth birthday on the way. Most young ladies already had gentlemen callers by their age. She turned back to the mirror and made a face at her red hair and freckled face. There was *her* reason. She didn't know what had been the problem for Abigail. Perhaps her childishness.

"I need to hurry," she said. "Mother expects me down in twenty minutes."

Abigail turned away reluctantly. A frown creased her forehead and she said with a pout, "You will tell me what happens. Promise?"

"Promise," agreed Cassie and turned back to her hair.

She did feel sorry for Abigail, but at the same time she reminded herself that she was sure there would be no invitation for her should Abigail's father, Mr. Jordan, ever decide to entertain young attorneys.

The new dinner guest was tall, blond, and had a most bewitching mustache. Cassie was quite taken with him and wished for one moment that Abigail had been there to see him for herself. Then she dismissed the thought. She had to stop thinking about Abigail and learn to be a part of the adult world.

On a few occasions she managed to enter the table conversation and it seemed that she committed no terrible blunders. She felt a bit heady with her accomplishment and even wished that the dinner hour might continue a bit longer. But as though on cue, as soon as the dessert was served, her father pushed back from the table, informed Dickerson that the men would have their coffee in the library, and excused himself and his guests from the table.

"Why don't we work in the drawing room for a while?" her mother asked as soon as she had excused the three boys.

Cassie nodded her agreement. She did not even feel annoyed at the suggestion.

"I thought dinner went very well, didn't you?" said Mrs. Winston when they were seated and had picked up their needlework.

Cassie looked up in surprise, noting her mother's calm, pleased look.

"You handled yourself very nicely in the conversation," her mother continued, and Cassie colored slightly at the compliment.

"You really are much more mature than Abigail. But when you are constantly together, I fear she has a way of holding you back."

Mrs. Winston went right on stitching. Cassie was not sure how to interpret the comment, whether to be annoyed or pleased.

She punched the needle through the linen with a bit more force than usual and stole a glance at her mother. But Mrs. Winston seemed to be neither upset nor reprimanding.

Cassie lowered her eyes again and carefully pressed the needle through the material.

"Dr. Sawyer seems like a nice young man," Mrs. Winston noted, changing the direction of the conversation.

Cassie flushed slightly, thinking of the blond head and the twitching mustache and nodded her head without comment.

"Too bad he is already engaged," her mother commented.

Cassie's hands went still in her lap.

"She is waiting for him back in Toronto. They are to be married as soon as he has finished his internship."

So that's that, thought Cassie, immediately shifting her thoughts back to Dr. Corouthers. *I'm as fickle as Abigail,* she chided herself and managed to prick her finger. "Ouch!" she exclaimed, her finger quickly moving to her lips.

"Remember your thimble," spoke her mother. "That is what it is for—to guard your fingers."

It was not much of a prick, but a little drop of blood was dotting the end of her finger.

"I suppose you will have to lay aside your work for tonight," her mother said, and added, "but you don't need to run up to your room. I like to have your company. Why don't you read by the fire—or just sit and chat."

Cassie had never been invited to sit and chat with her mother in the drawing room before. Oh, they had enjoyed little visits in her bedroom or on the porch swing when she had been younger. But then the years had seemed to send them both separate ways. Cassie had done her chatting with Abigail, and her mother had shared afternoon teas with lady friends. Now for some reason it seemed right that they share time together. Cassie laid aside her sewing but did not pick up a book.

"Have you decided what you would like to do for your birthday?" asked Mrs. Winston.

Cassie had spent many hours weaving elaborate plans of how she would celebrate her eighteenth birthday. She was about to begin spilling it all out to her mother when she realized just how childish her intentions had been—like something she might have wished to do when she turned twelve.

"Not really," she responded, stirring restlessly in her chair.

"Well, we have a couple weeks yet. I'm sure you'll think of something."

"I—I think I'd just like a—quiet dinner," Cassie surprised herself by saying.

"A quiet dinner?" Mrs. Winston sounded surprised. "With your father's friends?"

"No. No," said Cassie quickly. "Just us."

Mrs. Winston nodded. "I'm sure that can easily be arranged," she agreed, though her brow puckered slightly. "With Abigail?"

"I—I don't think so. Not for dinner. Perhaps—perhaps in the afternoon we could have some of my school friends in for tea."

Mrs. Winston smiled. "That's a wonderful idea," she enthused. "I will begin making the arrangements right away."

Cassie knew from years of experience that the "tea" would be done with an elegant flair. Her mother enjoyed afternoon teas and Cassie's friends were bound to be impressed.

———

The tea was perfect. All her friends told her so. Attractive gifts helped to make her little party a day to be cherished in memories.

The family dinner party was just as successful. Her mother and father both seemed pleased that she had chosen to have a family celebration. Even her brothers were quite awed and entered wholeheartedly in the spirit of the event.

I am now eighteen, thought Cassie later that evening as she unpinned her long tresses and let them spill over her shoulders. Then she lifted up the new emerald-green silk from her parents and studied her image in the mirror.

Mama is right. It does suit my coloring. She had noticed

that her mother had not said "red hair and freckles" but "coloring." It sounded so much better.

But the hair was still just as red, she noticed, though the gown did enhance her green eyes.

"Mama says the freckles are fading," she told her reflection, "but they are still there. I can see them. One here, another here, and one there—and there."

Cassie turned from her mirror, not wanting to count any more freckles.

"Abigail says she's heard of women who cover them up with face powder," she continued her soliloquy. "I must see if I can find some the next time I am shopping."

And feeling a little better about her appearance, Cassie carefully hung her new dress in the wardrobe and prepared for bed.

———————

Dr. Corouthers must know that I am now eighteen, Cassie thought in frustration. Her father's guests had been to dinner and were now ensconced in her father's study discussing medical things again. Cassie felt a bit of annoyance that no sign of an approach had been made to her father.

She had purchased the face powder and had come to an understanding with her mother as to how much a proper young lady might be free to use—but still the gentleman had not asked if he could call.

It's my red hair, she fumed silently. *He does not find it attractive.*

"I noticed that Dr. Corouthers pays you fine compliments," her mother spoke, interrupting her dark reverie.

Compliments, yes, Cassie wanted to respond, *but no inquiring if he might call. I am beginning to think he is just a flirt.*

Instead, she answered demurely, "He is a pleasant conversationalist," then turned their conversation to other things.

Cassie was about to lay aside her sewing and retire for

the night when her father entered the room. His brow was slightly puckered as though he had been caught off guard on some matter. Mrs. Winston looked up with concern in her eyes. He flashed a plea for help in her direction and then turned to Cassie.

"There is a young man in the library waiting to speak with you," he said, puzzlement on his face spilling over into his tone.

Cassie rose to her feet, sharing her father's confusion.

"He asked me if he could—but I said you are now of age and should speak for yourself," Dr. Winston went on.

Cassie stood bewildered, unsure whether to sit back down or move toward the door.

"Well, don't keep the young gentleman waiting, dear," Mrs. Winston urged, and Cassie looked at her mother to see a soft smile playing about her lips.

Cassie paled, then flushed. Her fingers trembled and her knees shook. *It has come. Dr. Corouthers is finally asking if he might call.* She'd had no idea that it would catch her so by surprise when it finally did happen. She had considered herself prepared. But now as she moved forward on wooden legs, her mouth dry and her cheeks flaming, she wondered why she had ever wanted him to ask in the first place. She wasn't ready. Not really.

But the die had been cast. Her father had not even answered on her behalf, which would have saved her much anguish. Oh, if only he had said a yes or a no, Cassie was sure she would cheerfully have consented to either.

She stopped in the hall, halfway between the drawing room and the library, and willed her pulse to stop racing and her breathing to return to normal. She practiced a few little smiles, hoping that they were demure, yet encouraging. She drew a big breath and proceeded to the library. Hoping that her cheeks were not flaming or her hands moist with perspiration, she pushed the door gently open, her warm smile firmly in place, and saw a man quickly rise to his feet.

She was facing Mr. Smith.

Chapter Six

Courting

Cassie's smile quickly faded. She paled, then blushed. "I'm—I'm dreadfully sorry. I thought—" She could not finish her statement. She obviously had misunderstood the entire situation.

Mr. Smith realized that something had gone amiss.

"Your father didn't tell you?" he asked softly, moving forward in case she needed a supporting hand.

"No. No, he—well, yes, he—he did say that someone was—was waiting," fumbled Cassie.

"Ah-h," said the perceptive Mr. Smith, his head lifting back. "But you didn't expect it to be me. Is that it?"

Cassie could feel her cheeks coloring again. She scarcely knew how to answer, but she had been taught to be honest. "Yes. Yes," she stammered, "I really wasn't expecting it to be you."

"I'm sorry," he responded quickly. "I—I do hope that you aren't too dreadfully disappointed."

Cassie sensed his embarrassing position. She shook her head and reached a hand out to him. "Oh, it isn't that—that way. It was just that I never—I never considered that you—that you might—might—?" She had no way of completing the statement.

"You thought that I could sit at the dinner table week after week, month after month, and not see for myself what

50

an attractive and intelligent and pleasant young woman you have become?"

His flattery caught her totally off guard and she trembled. "It's just—just that you are always so—so studious—so serious about—about your—your work, that I didn't think—"

He smiled, and Cassie was reminded again of the attractiveness of his smile and how it completely transformed his face. Her head was reeling, her body taut. Suddenly she felt the need to sit down. She was glad a chair was close by. He eased it under her as she began to sink. His hand rested lightly on her shoulder. She wondered if he was about to call her father.

"I'm—I'm fine," she managed, swallowing to try to take the dryness from her throat.

"Catch your breath for a moment," he cautioned. "Just take your time. Deep breaths. Now another. There. Another. Good. Your color is coming back nicely."

Cassie took some more deep breaths and the room stopped its spinning. He watched her closely for a few moments before removing his hand from her shoulder and walking a few paces away.

"I'm sorry," he said again as he turned to face her. "I—I didn't realize that any young lady would be so shocked that a gentleman would request to call."

He smiled again and Cassie wondered how she could ever have considered him plain.

"It's—it's just—just that—"

"I know. You thought I had interest only in my work," he repeated teasingly.

He sat on the edge of her father's broad desk and smiled at her again. She had never seen a person's eyes look so alive—so—so enchanting. But then she had paid little attention to his eyes. They were always hidden behind his wire-framed glasses.

She managed to nod her head and return a little smile. It was not demure. It was not particularly encouraging. It was a tentative offering of friendship—a sharing of a common experience and a little joke.

"Can we start over?" he asked candidly, and she was able to laugh and nod her head in agreement.

He stood again, his brow puckered slightly in seriousness. She noted that his fingers clasped and intertwined nervously. Suddenly she felt nervous no longer. His own agitation had eased hers.

"Shall I go out and come back in?" she asked with a teasing lift to her voice.

He responded with a nod of his head, and an amused look slightly curved his mouth. "Would you?" he asked.

"Of course," she replied. She stood to her feet and gave him a smile that turned shy as she left the room, closing the door softly behind her.

She stood for a few minutes trying to calm her racing heart, trying to get her trembling hands under control, then reached to push the door open, placed the nervous smile back on her face, and entered the room.

"Miss Winston," he said, advancing toward her and reaching for her hand. "I thank you for agreeing to see me."

She could not keep her smile from becoming soft laughter. He shared the joke, then continued. "I know I have done nothing in the past to show my feelings—but I have grown to admire you—and—" He paused long enough to draw in a quick breath. "I would be honored if you would allow me the privilege of calling."

"I—I would welcome—would be happy to—" Where were all the nice little speeches she had rehearsed so carefully for just such a moment? She felt like a schoolgirl again, tripping over her tongue in embarrassment. But he didn't seem to notice. The pressure of his fingers on her hand had increased.

"So it is agreed," he said with apparent relief. "I was afraid you might not consider me. I have not yet graduated. But I have just learned that my internship is to be served in Ottawa. If I didn't—didn't take advantage of my opportunity now—I—would most surely lose you to another. I couldn't risk that—you understand."

Cassie removed her hand and stood trembling. What had

she done? What was he saying? "I—I haven't agreed to marry you," she stammered bluntly. "I just—"

"Oh, I know—I know. I am sorry." He turned slightly and his face flushed as hers had a few moments earlier. "I am making a dreadful blunder of things," he admitted frankly. "I—I assure you—I am quite aware that you have made no promises. Please forgive me. I—I promise that I will be careful not to assume—more than you have—have been willing to grant me."

"A call," said Cassie. "A call!"

"Nothing more," he continued. "I feel—feel honored that you have agreed to let me call."

"And your studies?" prompted Cassie. She had lived with her father long enough to understand the importance of studies as one neared graduation.

"They will not suffer, I promise you. I would never jeopardize my training—not even—" He stopped and smiled at her again. "Not even for your pretty face."

Cassie returned the smile. It was hard not to respond to the way his whole face lighted up.

"Very well," she said and a bit of coyness crept in. She lowered her eyes and toyed with her lace hankie. A thought flashed through her mind. *At least now Dr. Corouthers will be forced to see that I am not a child.* She quickly pushed the thought aside. Somehow it seemed very childish indeed.

"When?" he was asking and Cassie had to bring her attention back to the moment at hand.

"When?"

"When might I call?"

She turned to him again and saw the eagerness in his eyes. He really was serious about it all.

"Well, I—I suppose that will partly depend upon your study load," she responded, stalling for time.

"Next Thursday? I have an exam to write that day. My studying will need to be completed beforehand. I would welcome a chance to—to relax and—and enjoy some company after the grind of the day."

Cassie lifted her eyes to look directly into his. They were

hazel. She had wondered. She had never been able to describe them. They were not blue, nor brown, nor green like her own. They were hazel—almost changing color along with his mood. Right now they shadowed, awaiting her answer.

"Next Thursday," she agreed and the hazel eyes began to sparkle.

———

"You what?" squealed Abigail.

"I agreed to allow Mr. Smith to call," repeated Cassie evenly.

"Smith? Why Smith? He is most ordinary. There is nothing—nothing outstanding about him."

Cassie's chin lifted in stubborn defense. "I disagree," she said firmly. "He has a delightful smile."

"A smile! And you are going to marry a man for his smile?"

"I didn't say I was going to marry him," protested Cassie angrily. "I said he is coming to call."

"But marriage comes after calling," countered Abigail.

"Not always," stated Cassie with a shake of her red head. "People court and—and end the relationship, all the time."

"You are just starting to court and you are already breaking up?" shrieked Abigail. "That's foolish."

"I didn't say I was breaking up," Cassie cast at her friend. "I said that I am allowing him to call. One makes up one's mind when the proper time comes."

She felt cross with Abigail. She was behaving so foolishly over the whole thing.

Abigail's fingers nervously twisted a knot in her cambric shawl. "It's just—just that we have—have always done things together," she said at length.

Now Cassie understood her friend's petulant mood. Her anger softening, she assured her, "He's only calling. It doesn't mean I'll be marrying and moving across town or anything. He's just calling."

She didn't say to Abigail that she was still hoping Dr.

Corouthers might also decide to call.

"He is very plain," Abigail insisted and her words brought a smile to Cassie's lips.

"Perhaps. Then again—it may be how one decides to look at him. He does have a lovely smile. And—and did you know his eyes are hazel? Quite attractive really. They change—they change colors according to his mood. They darken and then they—they light up. I have never seen eyes quite—"

"Only calling?" Abigail interrupted. "You say he is only calling—just as if you really don't care one way or the other, and yet you babble on and on about his—his eyes! I think you are smitten already."

She threw the last statement at Cassie and rose angrily from the chintz chair and flung herself toward the door.

"And I'll just bet you never once thought to remind Mr. Birdwell that I have had my eighteenth birthday," she hissed, and was gone, slamming the door behind her.

———

Mr. Smith arrived promptly at the appointed hour on Thursday. If Cassie had worried about the evening dragging, she needn't have. She was pleasantly surprised by the number of things they had to discuss and found Mr. Smith to be relaxed and an enjoyable companion. By the time the evening had ended with coffee and some of Cook's delicious tea cakes, Cassie was wishing they had a few more hours to spend together.

"May I accompany you to church on Sunday?" asked Mr. Smith and Cassie nodded her head in agreement without even thinking of Dr. Corouthers.

"Your folks will not object to your sitting with me instead of in the family pew?"

"I'm sure they won't," replied Cassie. "But if by chance they should, why don't you join us?"

"I'd love to," he hastened to assure, giving her one of his charming smiles.

"If the morning is pleasant, will you walk with me?"

"I'd like that," answered Cassie.

"I'll see you then. Nine-thirty or thereabout?"

"Nine-thirty should give us plenty of time," agreed Cassie.

He reached for her hand and for one minute she thought he might raise her fingers to his lips, but he pressed gently and released them. "Until Sunday," he whispered, then lifted his hat and proceeded down the broad boardwalk.

Cassie soon dismissed all thoughts of Dr. Corouthers during the next weeks and months. If she had stopped to think about him at all, she may have wondered what she found so attractive. He now seemed dreadfully old and terribly stodgy. And his smile was rather—rather pasted into place, not spontaneous and totally joyous and captivating.

Samuel Smith called as frequently as his heavy study schedule would allow. Cassie looked forward to the evenings they shared and was gloomy and restless when the visits were interrupted by his studies.

He had ceased being Mr. Smith—just as she had ceased being Miss Winston. His name was Sam, he had informed her, and he would be pleased if she would choose to use it. She felt Sam too plain for the man she had come to know, and announced decisively that she would call him Samuel. He smiled at that and indulged her in the matter. "And I shall call you Cassandra," he countered, and Cassie felt it was a fair exchange. No one else called her by her given name—not since school days when her teacher had spoken it with a prim and cool voice.

But Samuel did not speak her name with coldness. She heard a warmth unknown to her—not even from her father or mother. Soon Cassie was admitting to herself that she had indeed been enamored by soon-to-be Dr. Samuel Smith and his winning smile.

She was no longer a young girl in love with love. She was a young woman in love with a man.

As Samuel's graduation drew near, Cassie both looked

forward to it and dreaded it. She knew that Samuel might not feel free to speak of marriage until he was in a position to properly support a wife. On the other hand, his internship was to be served in Ottawa and that was many miles away. She hated to see him go. Hated to think of the long, lonely days without him. She consoled herself with the fact that she could spend those days preparing herself to be a proper wife for the man she intended to marry, for she had now made up her mind that marry him she would. And regardless of his time in internship, they could have a "promise" in place.

But as the days ticked past too quickly, Samuel still did not speak of marriage, and Cassie often wished she were free to bring up the subject herself.

"Bother!" she exclaimed to herself one evening after he had left. "Why does society put such ridiculous restrictions on women? I know he loves me. I know he is thinking of marriage every bit as much as I am. So why can't we talk about it?"

She pulled her shawl from her shoulders with an angry jerk and tossed it on her bed.

"If it were up to me, we would have this out in the open and settled," she went on. "No use pretending that we haven't considered the idea. There are plans to be made. Things to be decided. But oh no. A man's honor is at stake. He can't discuss such a thing until he is 'financially sound.' Ridiculous!"

But each time Samuel called, Cassie laid aside her irritation and pretended to be the innocent young woman, totally oblivious to her charms and the love of the man who came calling.

But her heart became more and more agitated as the graduation date approached. What if she had misread things? What if Samuel would just walk out of her life? What if her first little speech about "calling only" were taken seriously by the serious young man? What if he hadn't realized she had changed in her feelings toward him since that night long ago? Cassie trembled at the thought and wondered if she would be able to hold her tongue and let Samuel Smith walk away.

Chapter Seven

Sharing Dreams

Cassie attended the graduation ceremonies with her mother. Her father was on the platform, prepared to make a speech and award the new medical doctors their degrees. Cassie smiled as she watched Samuel cross the platform. He had made it—and in fine form, too. Her father beamed as he passed his protege the diploma.

Now we can make our plans, Cassie told herself. But even as she thought the words, she fidgeted. It was only four days until Samuel would be boarding the train for Ottawa. There wasn't much time for discussing plans.

A little celebration at the Winston home followed the ceremonies. Cassie served punch and coffee, irritation tainting her usual good graces. She was anxious for the other guests to leave so she and Samuel might settle in the parlor and get down to some serious talking.

By the time the last guest had taken leave, it was getting late. One glimpse at Samuel, and Cassie realized he was exhausted.

"You look dreadfully tired," she said in sympathy.

"It's all that final cramming," he admitted. "And today was a strain, I do admit."

"You'd better get some sleep," she said with understanding.

"Do you mind?"

"Of course I mind," she responded, but she tried to cover

the words with a smile. "We can talk tomorrow."

At Samuel's frown, Cassie realized there was some reason why tomorrow might not work out either.

"Is there something wrong?" she asked frankly.

"No, not wrong—but I do have a million things I must attend to tomorrow. You do understand?"

"Of course," replied Cassie, but her eyes dropped to the tray she still held in her hands.

Samuel reached out a finger and lifted her chin so she was forced to raise her eyes to his. "You do understand?" he pressed.

Cassie managed a smile. "You have only four days," she whispered and let her eyes drop again. Her lips were trembling and she feared she might burst into tears.

"Four days is a long time," he promised, coaxing her to smile again.

She tried. She lifted her eyes to his and did manage a wobbly smile in response to his prompting.

"That's my girl," he said softly and Cassie's smile deepened.

"I'll be around as quickly as I can get here, day after tomorrow," he promised, and Cassie knew it would have to do.

"Now—you get a good sleep. We have a lot of talking to do."

With that promise he left her and Cassie moved about in a dream. Surely she had understood his meaning. Before he left for Ottawa they would have their future plans settled.

She went to bed but could not get to sleep. *If only Abigail were here to share my secret,* she mused, then dismissed the thought. She did not want to share this special joy even with her best friend. She hugged it to herself and savored the feeling. She was soon to become Mrs. Dr. Samuel Smith. Or was it Dr. Mrs. Samuel Smith? She could not untangle the name. Her mother always went by Mrs. Henry P. Winston. She finally settled on being Mrs. Samuel J. Smith. That was quite good enough.

It was almost morning before she finally settled into sleep. By then she was exhausted—but happy. She hoped the coming day would pass quickly so she could sleep through another night and bring Samuel to her side.

The day managed to drag, and because Cassie had not slept well and was already in a state of agitation, she was not good company. She fussed and fiddled and scolded the boys and criticized the household help. Her mother, sensing her frustration, suggested she visit a downtown shop.

"You need a new summer hat—why don't you shop for one?" was the way she put her proposal to Cassie. Cassie was only too glad for an excuse to escape.

"Can I take Abigail to help with the selection?" she asked, as if she were once again a small child asking for a favor.

"By all means," responded her mother. "Take Abigail. The walk will do you both good."

"Walk? I thought we'd take the carriage."

"Why don't you walk? The day will pass more quickly if you do."

Cassie nodded, though without real agreement, and went to ring Abigail on the phone. Soon the two of them were off toward the town shops, while Mrs. Winston heaved a sigh of relief and returned to her sewing.

It did help to fill in the day. The girls strolled into town, not hurrying, talking as they went. By the time they had visited their favorite milliners, agreed on a new hat for Cassie and returned home, the day was well spent. Abigail hurried on home so as not to be late for dinner, and Cassie climbed the stairs to freshen up for the evening meal.

That evening Cassie did not sit in the drawing room and sew with her mother. Instead, she excused herself and retired early.

She did manage to get to sleep even though she still felt agitated and restless. In her thinking, the only way to make the night pass and the new day dawn was to sleep it away.

The next morning she awakened to a drizzling sky. "I do wish God had arranged a nicer day," she grumbled to herself and then remembered she had not thought to ask Him for one. "I'm sorry," she whispered contritely. "I didn't mean to complain. It seems that I've been doing a good deal of complaining lately." Cassie tried to still her restless heart. "It's just—just this 'not knowing.' Not being able to make definite plans. I—I can't manage uncertainties very well. You know that."

She paused. "I'll be fine once Samuel gets here," she promised God and hastened to prepare herself for her friend's coming.

He did not keep her waiting. Just as he had promised, he arrived early in the forenoon. He had to shake rain from his hat and coat before he entered the hall, but he did not complain about the inclement weather as Cassie had done.

"Come to the parlor," Cassie urged. "Dickerson has laid a fire. You need to dry out. I'll fetch some coffee," and Cassie ushered Samuel to the parlor and hurried off to the kitchen.

They would have talked right through the lunch hour had not Stephen been sent to call them. Reluctantly they joined the family at the dining table.

The afternoon was again spent in conversation. They chatted easily, but Cassie began to get agitated again. It seemed that this visit was really getting them nowhere in particular.

They joined the family for dinner, then spent the evening before the open fire. The rain had ended by the time Samuel looked at his pocket watch and took his leave. Cassie hated to see him go. *Two days,* her heart kept crying, *two days and you'll be off to Ottawa. Shouldn't we make our plans?*

But Samuel seemed not to share her concern. The talk did not get around to settling things between them.

Samuel did not arrive again until late in the afternoon the next day. He brought Cassie up-to-date on his packing and planning. It seemed as if things were falling nicely into place for Samuel. He would soon be Dr. Smith, doing his internship at the Ottawa General. And she, Cassie, would be Cassandra Dell Winston, old maid back in Montreal.

Cassie bade Samuel a rather cool good-night when he left that evening. Tomorrow he would board his train and he still hadn't discussed their future together.

"You will go to the train with me, won't you?" he asked her, lifting her chin as he had a habit of doing.

Cassie nodded. She couldn't imagine not going to see him off.

"We need to talk," he whispered confidentially and leaned to kiss her cheek.

Cassie lingered in the hall. She didn't understand him at all. If he needed to talk, why didn't he talk? She had been there and she had been listening.

Reluctantly she climbed the steps to her room. Tomorrow was the final day. Tomorrow would be his last chance to ask her.

————

Her father suggested that she use the carriage and go around to pick up Samuel and take him to the train depot. Cassie was happy to comply with the arrangements. She called Samuel on the phone and told him that she would be there promptly at ten. That would give plenty of time for him to load his belongings and drive leisurely to the station. Any talking would have to be done in the privacy of the carriage on the way.

It wasn't the way Cassie would have planned it. Hardly the romantic setting she had envisioned for her proposal of marriage. But she told herself that any proposal was romantic and the time and place didn't really matter that much.

She arrived in front of Samuel's lodgings promptly at ten, and her driver helped Samuel load his trunk and carpetbags. Then Samuel climbed in beside her and they started off for the station. He was quiet and thoughtful for the first few moments, and Cassie feared he would never find his tongue. Then he reached for her hand and pressed it to his lips. "I'm really going to miss you," he whispered. "I pray that the days might pass quickly."

Cassie felt the tears gathering in her eyes.

"You have no idea how special the last few months have been to me," he went on. "I only wish I hadn't needed to keep my nose so closely in the books."

Cassie lifted a linen hankie and blew her nose softly.

"I don't know if I've ever told you how much it means to me to be able to get my medical training," he went on. When Cassie offered no comment, he continued. "My mother always planned that I should be a doctor and she set aside a little money as she could for my education. When she died, I wasn't sure if I still wanted to be a doctor. I guess I was just plain angry about her dying. And then I realized that if she had been where a doctor was available, she might not have died. That made me more determined than ever that I'd fulfill her dream."

He was silent for a few moments and then went on. "I don't know if I would have made it without the help of your father. He's a special man, Cassandra. A very special man. I owe so much to him—and I plan to pay him back by being the best doctor I can possibly be."

The horses had been passing through the streets at a brisk trot. Cassie glanced around her and realized they had only a few more blocks to go to reach the railway station. Panic caused her heart to begin to pound. He was talking—but not about the right things.

"Will you write me?" he was asking and Cassie could have shaken him. Of course she would write him. He need not have wasted their time asking.

"The time will pass," he continued. "I know it will drag for me—but I'll have my practice and you'll have your—"

What? she wanted to cut in. *What are you leaving for me? Your memory?*

But he continued. "—your family and friends—the church. The days will pass. Before we both know it the internship will be over and we will be free to make plans—"

"We are almost there," Cassie interrupted. The station was looming into view.

He tightened his grip on her hand.

"Your mother says that you are getting to be a fine cook," he said in lighter mood and Cassie pulled her hand away. She wasn't in a frame of mind to be teased.

"I might get some days off at Christmas. If I do, could I come to see you?"

"Of course," agreed Cassie, but reminded herself that Christmas was several months away.

The driver had pulled the horses to a halt and was slowly climbing down from the carriage seat. Samuel seized her hand again and pressed a kiss into her palm. "I'm going to miss you so much," he whispered and then he was stepping down from the carriage to help the driver with the trunk.

Cassie sat in frustration. *He is leaving*. Leaving just like that. Leaving with a promise of making plans when he completes his internship. *But that is way down the road*. What was she to do while he did his internship? What plans would she be able to make? How was she to spend her days—her hours? Waiting? Wondering?

She climbed stiffly from the carriage and walked with him into the station. She stood back and fidgeted while he purchased his ticket and checked the luggage. She fumed inwardly when he moved forward with a smile and held his hand out to her again.

"Walk with me to the platform?" he asked her.

She didn't answer, just trudged along at his side.

The train was hissing noisily as they made their way to the steps for boarding. He turned to her then and pulled her gently into his arms. She was sure he would say something. Ask her if she would wait for him. Tell her he wanted to marry her. But he said nothing. Just looked deeply into her eyes, then leaned to kiss her softly on the lips.

"Goodbye, Cassandra," he whispered against her hair. "I—I'm really going to miss you."

She thought she saw tears forming in his hazel eyes. They looked dark with sorrow, dark and brooding. She reached up to clasp the hand that brushed her cheek and then her tears began to spill unashamedly. He bent to kiss one of them away and then turned from her and hastened to board the train. In a moment he appeared at the window directly above her. She heard the grinding as he lifted the framed glass that separated them.

Already the train was hissing with renewed vigor and she knew it would soon be moving him down the tracks.

He leaned out the window and said another goodbye. She saw that he was about to lower the window again.

"Just a minute," she called into the noise about them.

He lifted the window higher and leaned out farther, cupping his hand to his ear so that he might hear her.

"Are you going to ask me to marry you or aren't you?" she screamed as loudly as she could.

She knew he had understood her by the shocked look on his face.

"Well—?" she yelled again. "Are you?"

"We need to talk," he hollered back at her. "We have so much to decide."

But Cassie was not to be put off. The train began to move slowly down the tracks and Cassie walked right along beside it, looking up at the window where Samuel stretched out to hear her.

"Are you?" she insisted again. "Because if you are, I'm saying yes."

People around them were grinning but Cassie paid no heed. She continued to walk alongside the train, her face turned upward toward Samuel.

"You'd say yes?" he called down to her, excitement showing in his face.

"Yes. I'm saying yes."

He stretched even farther from the train. For one terrifying moment she feared he might fall.

"Cassandra Winston," he shouted, "I love you. Will you marry me?"

Cassie forgot to walk. She stopped dead-still, her hands flying up to her face. He had said he loved her. He had proposed.

The train moved on without her, slowly gathering speed. Samuel was being borne quickly away. Suddenly she realized she had not answered him. She cupped her hands to her mouth. "Yes!" she cried as loudly as she could. "Yes, I will!" And she touched a finger to her lips to throw him a kiss and then stood with the tears streaming down her cheeks as she watched the train carry away the man she loved.

Chapter Eight

Letters

"My dearest Cassandra,

"You don't know how happy you have made me by promising to be my wife. I haven't been able to think of anything else since my departure from Montreal.

"I can't begin to count the number of times that I longed to speak to you about marriage, but it seemed so unfair to ask you to wait while I finished my internship."

Cassie flipped her red hair and said to herself, *Pawsh*, then continued reading.

"I feel there are so many things that we haven't yet discussed. Things pertaining to our future. I always want to be totally honest with you so that you will make the decision knowing full well what you are getting yourself into.

"You know I am from the West and you know that I want, more than anything else (except to marry you, of course), to practice medicine. I don't know if I have fully explained my intention of returning to Alberta for my practice."

Cassie drew in a deep breath and lowered the letter. "The West?" she exclaimed under her breath. "Why, it is a savage frontier. Pagan! How could—?"

She looked back at the pages that hung limply from her fingers, then raised them to go on with her reading.

"I know that Alberta is still a new land, rugged and rough, and not like the city you are used to. In fact, we would not even be in a city, for I plan to set up practice in the community where I grew up. That was my main reason for holding back in speaking to you of marriage.

"I know that you have been used to a fine home and all the amenities of life. I cannot promise you those things. At least not yet.

"For this reason I want you to think carefully before considering being my wife. If you should change your mind, I will understand and not hold it against you. Please think about this thoroughly and spend much time in prayer over the matter and I shall do likewise. This is not a light decision that I am asking you to make."

"I've already made my decision," said Cassie with a lift of her chin. "And I have no intention of changing it. But *Alberta*? We'll see."

The letter went on to tell of Samuel's new boardinghouse, the city, the hospital where he would soon begin his work. "I haven't been on duty yet," he continued, "but I did slip over to 'spy out' the place. It appears to be quite up-to-date and the staff that I met seem congenial. I am looking forward to getting started."

Cassie's eyes quickly scanned the rest of the message until they came to the words, "I love you and already miss you more than I can say. Please pray and seek God's direction for our future plans and take all the time you need to really know your heart. (Though I shall live in anguish until I know your answer.) But I promise not to press you on the matter.

"I will be waiting for your letter. I have enclosed my postal address. The mail is slow so I will try not to be too impatient. I do pray that the days and weeks pass quickly so that I might see you again.

"With my deepest devotion, Samuel."

Cassie sighed deeply as she lowered the letter. Then she held it to her bosom for a moment while the tears gathered in her eyes. She brushed them away with an impatient gesture and reread the last paragraphs of the letter. Then with determination she walked to her desk, seated herself, and took up pen and paper.

"My dear Samuel," she wrote, "I received your letter by

morning post and was pleased to hear that your train trip went well and you are nicely settled in your new place of residence.

"The days have been dragging for me since your departure. Mama tries to keep my hands occupied, but my mind is not so easily engaged. I think of you each hour of the day and pray that God will make your internship both pleasurable and profitable for you.

"As to the question of returning to Alberta, I believe the Bible states that one is to follow one's chosen companion, wherever God should lead him. If He leads you back to your West, then I assume that the West will be right for me also."

Cassie laid aside her pen and her forehead puckered slightly. Was she being totally honest? Did she really plan to travel west and live in an uncivilized country? She could not imagine the horrors it might hold.

"Yes. Yes," she said after a few moments of deep thought. "If that is what he really wants, I will go. I have learned to love him. I have no intention of losing him. But—but I do hope and pray that he doesn't decide to practice medicine in the West for the rest of his life—the rest of *our* lives."

And Cassie picked up her pen and continued her long, newsy letter.

————

As the weeks and months slipped slowly by, Samuel dared to accept the fact that Cassandra would really become his bride upon completion of his internship, and plans flew back and forth via letters.

"This is totally unfair to you," he said in one epistle, "to be courted by mail. A young, beautiful woman such as you should have a beau who can take you to concerts, plays, and picnics. Be there to accompany you to church and fairs. Bring you candy and flowers. And instead you must sit at home alone and be content to read letters that try, unsuccessfully, to express my heart."

Cassie pondered his statement. She hadn't exactly been

staying home alone. She still attended concerts and plays and even went on picnics. But she went with Abigail, who was still bemoaning the fact that Cassie was actually betrothed. Occasionally she went with her parents. And on rare and special occasions, her brother Stephen accompanied her.

"Do not fuss about the long-distance courtship," Cassie wrote back to Samuel. "I do miss you terribly and wish with all my heart that you could be here to do the things you described. But I am still getting out. Just the other night Stephen and I took in a play at the Opera House. He has really changed in the past year and Mama and Papa now allow him to escort me to some events."

At times Cassie could hardly believe that her brother—the pest—had seemed overnight to have become a young man, and a young man whose company she could enjoy.

"It used to be that I thought him a dreadful burden," her pen continued, "and now I have discovered that I shall actually miss him when I move away.

"Abigail and I go out together. She is still not being courted and it is terribly hard on her. She blames her father for not encouraging young suitors to call. He is a very opinionated man, I'm afraid, and I suppose he feels that no young man is good enough for his daughter. Mr. Birdwell, or I should now say Dr. Birdwell, Abigail's hopeful, has disappeared to who-knows-where. Abigail has completely lost touch."

Cassie dipped her pen in the ink well and thought of Abigail. She was having such a difficult time since Cassie was engaged. It certainly wasn't that Abigail was unattractive. Cassie remembered her own previous twinges of jealousy over Abigail's looks and now Cassie felt sorry for her.

By the time she resumed her letter, the ink on the pen tip had dried and she had to dip it again.

"We had our first snowfall a few nights ago," she continued. "Some of the young people from church are talking of a sleigh ride. Mama feels that it will be socially acceptable for me to join them if I have Stephen as an escort. Does it bother you at all if I go on such outings? I do not want to do anything that would offend."

And so the months passed and the letters continued. Samuel did not make it for Christmas as he had hoped. "I only get one day off," he wrote. "Other staff have seniority of course, and we are asked to be on duty almost around the clock. I am dreadfully disappointed. I had hoped so to see you again. I will be thinking of you—continually—and I hope that you will spare me a few moments of thought as well."

As soon as she had finished reading his letter, Cassie wiped away tears of disappointment, placed her new winter-gray bonnet on her red curls, and reached for her heavy coat.

"I am going shopping for Samuel," she informed her mother. "He isn't able to make it for Christmas and I wish to get a parcel off to him."

Her mother nodded in understanding and Cassie left the house to walk to the nearest shop.

It was a crisp winter day and the snow crunched underfoot with each step, and little puffs of cloud preceded her down the icy walk with each breath. The walk was good for her, the chill invigorating. By the time she had finished her purchases, she was in much better spirits. She hoisted her parcels and started for home.

"I will surprise him by sending baking done by my own hand," she planned as she walked briskly. She was confident now of her cooking. She was glad that her mother had insisted she learn. It was a good feeling to be able to account for oneself in the kitchen—even if one really did never need the skill.

"Has Papa said anything about finding a position for Samuel?" Mrs. Winston asked Cassie one evening as the two of them sat before the open fire, needlework in hand.

Cassie raised her head and looked at her mother, surprise widening her eyes.

"Samuel plans to go back to Alberta to practice," she replied slowly.

From the look of sheer horror that crossed her mother's

face, Cassie could tell that it was something she had not considered.

"You didn't know?" asked Cassie softly.

"Why, no. Why, I never would have suspected such a thing. A—a promising young doctor like him. Why, Papa is sure that he could do very well for himself in a city practice."

"I'm sure he could," replied Cassie with a touch of pride. "He has said that there have already been hints of his being offered a place in Ottawa."

"You—you knew his plans?" asked Mrs. Winston.

Cassie nodded. Her fingers moved deftly to ply the needle through the piece of silk she held in her hands.

"And you agreed?" Mrs. Winston seemed to think the idea preposterous.

"I agreed," replied Cassie.

Mrs. Winston dropped the needlework in her lap, her hands moving restlessly as though greatly agitated.

"Child, have you any idea what you have agreed to?" she asked at last.

Cassie raised her head high, hair glistening in the light of the parlor lamp. "I have agreed to marry the man I love," she said evenly.

"But—"

"Didn't you say that when one marries, one follows?"

"Well certainly but—"

"Well, I intend to do just that."

Mrs. Winston had no argument. She sat silently, trying to take in what her daughter had just spoken.

"Besides," said Cassie with a tilt to her head and a smile playing mischievously about her lips, "men have been known to change their minds before."

Mrs. Winston's breath caught in a little gasp. "Cassie, you wouldn't?" she began. "It isn't fair to promise one thing and plan another. It—it is deceitful and one must never begin a marriage with deceit."

Cassie's smile quickly faded and annoyance clouded her face. "Oh, Mama!" she exclaimed. "I am not being deceitful. If he wishes to stay in the West, I will stay in the West—but should he deem it wise to return to the East, I certainly will not forestall him."

Mrs. Winston still looked uncomfortable.

"It is a dangerous business to agree to a marriage where one is not in total accord," she warned her headstrong daughter.

"I am in accord, Mama. Please—don't fuss. I know what I'm doing. I love Samuel." And Cassie's eyes began to tear.

"I—I know. At least, I think I know. You do seem to be in love, but—but, my dear—you must think clearly—honestly—for your sake and for his. Do you love him enough?"

Cassie laid aside her work and stood to her feet. She reached in a pocket for a lace hankie and touched it to her welling eyes. "I love him, Mama," she said firmly. "I love him. And I have thought about it, and I have prayed about it."

Mrs. Winston nodded her head slowly. "Then I suggest," she said carefully, "that both of us consider the West to be your future home—since that is Samuel's intent."

Cassie wheeled away from her mother and left the room with a swishing of skirts. It was the first quarrel she'd had with her mother for many months and she suddenly felt like a child again. It was unfair. Totally unfair. Why didn't her mother leave her to work out her own future? After all, it was up to her and to Samuel. They were old enough to know their own minds. Weren't they?

They were married in a quiet, yet beautiful ceremony one week after Samuel had completed his internship. Mrs. Winston was in her element, planning and organizing all the details of the wedding and reception. Abigail was Cassie's sole attendant, while Stephen stood with Samuel.

Mrs. Winston used up three handkerchiefs during the ceremony, and Dr. Henry P. was forced to clear his throat many times. Their little girl had grown up and made a beautiful bride, the brilliant color of her hair softened by a white tulle veil and her wide-skirted white gown emphasizing her brilliantly shining green eyes and her creamy skin—almost devoid of freckles.

"She does look happy," Mrs. Winston had to admit, but was there a hint of a nagging little fear in her eyes?

The honeymoon was a very short affair, only two days spent at Niagara Falls, and then they returned to Montreal and busied themselves with the task of packing and planning for their trip west.

Cassie became more and more aware of Samuel's excitement. *He can hardly wait,* she mused. *He can hardly wait to get back to Alberta.* In spite of herself, Cassie had been secretly entertaining the hope that Samuel might decide to accept her father's invitation to join him in his well-established Montreal practice.

"I really have more than I can carry," her father had said in her hearing. "With the practice and the teaching, there are not enough hours in my day. I already am refusing new admissions. With the two of us, the practice could be expanded to keep us both as busy as we wish to be."

Samuel, looking dreadfully uncomfortable, had cleared his throat. He had just been honored by the man he esteemed most highly. The man who was also the father of his wife. And yet his heart and soul was in the West. He twisted uncomfortably in his seat and Cassie held her breath. For one moment she wished to cut in and tell her father that Samuel had already made up his mind and shouldn't be pushed for a difficult decision. Then she swallowed the words and prayed inwardly that Samuel might find it in his heart to accept her father's offer without feeling compromised.

But Samuel was speaking, slowly, deliberately. "I cannot express my deep appreciation for your offer, sir. There is no one—no one—that I would sooner practice with."

Cassie let out her breath. He was going to do it. Going to stay in Montreal. She wanted to squeal—to clap her hands childishly. She half rose to go to Samuel—but he was still speaking.

"The truth is, sir, that I have made a promise to myself. You see, my mother died because there was no doctor to attend her. She left a family of three little ones and a broken-hearted husband. That sort of thing is repeated over and over in the West. Mothers taken, babies lost, families bereft of fathers before their time. I—I can't stop it all, sir, but I might prevent one or two. Just one or two and my work will be rewarded, my life worthwhile. I know it won't be easy—for me—and especially for Cassandra." He turned and reached for her hand as he spoke the words, and Cassie responded by holding tightly to his hand. "But she knows. She is a brave, courageous woman, and I feel that she is strong enough, in body and spirit, to join me. If I wasn't confident of that, I would never have asked her to be my wife."

Her father sat back in his big leather chair and cleared his throat. He did not speak for many minutes. Instead, he sat gazing off into space as though carefully considering the statement made by the man before him.

He cleared his throat again and stood to face his son-in-law. Then he extended his hand and clasped the strong one of the young doctor.

"I can only say, God bless you, son." Tears glistened in his eyes, and he reached a hand to squeeze Samuel's shoulder firmly, then turned and quietly left the room.

Cassie had never seen her father weep before and the experience unnerved her. She wasn't sure if he was weeping because her husband had refused him, because he was losing a cherished daughter, or simply because he was touched by the fervor of the younger doctor. Her body began to tremble and she wished to take flight. Then Samuel was drawing her into the circle of his arms and kissing her hair and her cheeks, and she decided that she was exactly where she wanted to be.

Chapter Nine

A New Life

The train ride west was long and boring. There was very little of interest for Cassie to see.

Samuel was not much help, for he had his nose buried in a medical book Dr. Henry P. had given him upon his departure. Now and then he raised his head to smile at his new bride or to lovingly pat her hand, but quickly returned to his reading. Cassie yawned and again looked out the window at the vast expanse of prairie grass waving in the continuous wind.

They did pass through small towns. Settlements really, and Cassie felt the alarm growing within her.

"Is Calgary like this?" she asked, referring to a shack-filled hamlet with streets rutted from recent rain, and yards devoid of anything growing.

Samuel laid aside his book and reached for her hand. "Calgary is much bigger," he assured her, "and much more—more settled and civil."

Cassie breathed a sigh of relief and reminded herself that they would not be living in Calgary.

"What about Jaret?" she asked him.

Samuel waited for a moment before answering her question, wanting to be honest—yet encouraging. "Jaret is much smaller than Calgary," he admitted. "But it isn't as rugged as the town we just saw."

"I should hope not," replied Cassie in relief, but she did

not see the concerned look that darkened her husband's eyes.

He held her hand tightly.

"It really is quite—quite different from what you are used to," he said softly. "There are no operas, no plays, no fancy shops or paved streets. They are not even cobbled. Just hard-packed prairie soil. You will have many adjustments."

"A church?" she asked glumly.

"A little community church," he answered.

Cassie nodded, thankful they had that much. At least, the place would not be totally heathen.

"You will be seen as the community—well—leader. You and the local minister's wife."

Cassie had never thought of that before and the idea pleased her. It would be rather exciting to be the one to bring culture to a frontier town. She could hardly wait for Samuel to return to his book so she might commence her planning. Where would she begin? With opera? No, that would come later. Perhaps with plays. They were much easier to handle and might even be able to use some locals—in lesser roles, of course. Perhaps she herself could take the lead. She might even write the script herself. That would be rather fun. They could do one presentation prior to Christmas and another at the Easter season. They could start with stories based on biblical characters. That way the people would be entertained and taught at the same time. Perhaps even the Indians could be invited to attend.

With that thought Cassie leaned forward quickly and grasped Samuel's sleeve. He looked up from his book.

"Samuel," she asked sharply, fear and agitation edging her voice, "are there Indians in Jaret?"

He nodded, a puzzled look furrowing his brow.

"Are they—safe?" she asked, her green eyes wide with horror.

He smiled, a slow amused smile, and his hazel eyes looked almost blue behind his wire-rimmed glasses.

"Quite!" was his simple answer.

He brushed the ever-straying thatch of thick brown hair back from his forehead, and Cassie felt that for a moment he looked quite boyish. A surge of love for him passed through her being and she reached for his hand again. Her cultural plans for the town would have to wait. For the moment she wished to give her full attention to her husband.

She had been pleasantly surprised with Calgary. Oh, it certainly could not measure up to Montreal, but there was a newness, a vigor about the small city that drew her. And she did find the mountains to the west very appealing.

Never had she seen streets so a-bustle with activity. Never had she seen such a diversity of humankind. She wished she could openly stare at all she saw, but good breeding demanded she mask her curiosity.

"How long can we stay here?" she asked Samuel, hoping his answer would assure her they were due for a long, long stay.

"We should have things arranged in a couple of days," he said instead. "Three at the most."

"How do we get to Jaret?" she asked then. "By train?"

"I need a buggy and some good horses," he informed her. "I hope to buy them here. We'll drive to Jaret."

"I thought it was miles away," she told him.

"It is—but within driving distance. Folks make the trip without giving it a thought."

Cassie was not sure she'd make the trip without thought. What would they ever do if they should be overtaken by Indians on the trail? She looked around nervously. She saw a few people on the streets who were decidedly different from the folks she was accustomed to seeing. Some of them might even be Indians. Perhaps, even now, they were eying the newcomers to see if it would be worth their while to lift a scalp or two. She shivered and walked closer to Samuel.

They stayed in a hotel in the heart of downtown, and Cassie found it to be quite adequate—if not elegant. She was left on her own for hours at a time while Samuel made his purchases and cared for their travel plans.

In the evenings he took her to restaurants in the city, and she found the outings exciting in spite of her discomfort with the strangeness. One evening they even attended a play following dinner, and to her surprise the audience was well behaved and the presentation much better than she had dared expect.

"I can't believe it," she said to Samuel. "They had costumes and fine sets and everything." To which Samuel only smiled.

On the third day Samuel said they were ready to travel. It had taken him a bit longer than he had planned to make all his purchases and arrangements.

"We won't leave now until morning," he informed Cassie. "I just hope the weather holds."

Cassie wasn't sure about the weather. It felt dreadfully hot to her. She was glad for the relative comfort of her hotel room.

He awakened her—far too early, she thought—the next morning and hurried her as she did her final packing. Then they partook of an early breakfast, gathered the packed lunch, loaded the last of their belongings, and started off toward the south, seeming to follow the gentle curve of the Rocky Mountains.

Samuel had hired a driver and wagon to transport much of their belongings, and he settled into position in the new bennet buggy with Cassie at his side just as the sun came over the horizon. To her amazement the streets of the city were already bustling with activity.

"My, folks do get up early here," she observed sleepily.

"Most folks have a long way to travel," responded Samuel and clucked to the bay that pulled their springed carriage.

It was chilly in the early hours of the morning, but before long Cassie laid aside her shawl. The day grew increasingly warmer with each passing hour, until Cassie was thankful for any light breeze that might give them a bit of air.

In the afternoon after they had stopped to partake of the picnic lunch, storm clouds gathered, and Cassie felt relieved to be out of the sun. But Samuel kept his eyes on the sky.

"I don't think we're going to make it," he said at last. "The storm is moving in quickly."

Just as he finished speaking, the first raindrops began to fall. There was no place to go for shelter. They were in the open without even the benefit of trees.

Samuel pulled the bay mare to a halt and reached in the back of the buggy, drawing forward a rough, odorous tarp.

"Wrap this around you," he instructed and Cassie turned, aghast at the thought.

"You're going to get soaked clear through if you don't," he warned her, and Cassie reluctantly allowed him to wrap them both in the smelly canvas. She soon found that Samuel was right. The skies seemed to open above them and pour out their contents with a vengeance. The once-dry and dusty track soon became a muddy bog, and the bay mare labored under the weight of the small buggy.

The wagon that followed them was forced to pull over to the side of the trail to wait out the storm. Already the team was breathing heavily, their full sides heaving with the exertion of the pull.

"No use wearying the team," Samuel called to the driver. "I'll go on ahead and find shelter for Mrs. Smith."

Even with the tarp wrapped around her, Cassie was unable to keep dry. She could feel the water seeping through in a dozen different places. She felt cold and miserable and terribly unattractive. The bay mare trudged on through the mud and rainfall until they were all spattered and wet. As they were turning into a crude farmyard, Cassie suddenly remembered she was wearing her best bonnet. With a cry of alarm she snatched it from her head, not even taking the time to undo the pins.

As she held the sodden bit of blue felt in her hands, the tears welled up in her eyes. It was ruined! Totally ruined and she had planned to use the stylish hat as her first offering of refinement and culture to the new community.

"It's only a hat," Samuel said beside her, and Cassie crumbled the wet headdress in her hands and began to sob.

Samuel realized, too late, that he had said the wrong thing.

"We'll get you another one," he tried to console her. "The next time we're in Calgary. You won't need hats as much in Jaret anyway."

But his well-intentioned words held no comfort for Cassie. She clung to her ruined bonnet and continued to cry.

Samuel drove the mare as close to the rough building as he could. Cassie noticed that there was smoke coming from a simple chimney pipe. Then the door swung open and a man, his suspenders drooping and his red underwear showing as his upper garment, stood in the doorway. A stubby pipe was clamped in his teeth and he puffed away as he stood looking at his visitors.

"Come in," he called through clenched teeth. "It's a real soaker."

Without a word Samuel climbed from the buggy and reached up for Cassie's hand. She still clutched her ruined blue felt and refused to let it go even to assist her descent from the wagon.

She did manage to sniff and wipe away her tears. She felt sure that the man in the door would not be able to pick out tears from raindrops, and for the moment she did not care in the least if he could.

It was warm in the small cabin—for that Cassie was thankful. She was even wetter than she had known, and her sodden skirts clung to her legs as she tried to move.

"Put yer hoss in the barn," the man was offering, and Cassie was aware that Samuel moved off to somewhere, leaving her totally alone with the whiskered old gent.

He turned around and pushed the door closed with a heave of his shoulder, leaving the room in darkness. There was only the dim light coming from one small smoke-filmed window and the flickering flame from the open fire.

"Looks like the storm caught ya off guard," he observed. "Here. Hustle up to the fire and dry yerself off."

Cassie accepted the chair he offered. Her limp skirts dragged about her feet. In her hand she still held the bonnet, shapeless and dripping and totally ruined.

Then she felt her hair begin to tumble down around her

face. She had dislodged it when she had pulled at the hat.

What a sight I must be, she thought, the tears threatening to spill again. *I do hope there's no woman in this house to see me like this.*

She released the treasured bit of felt, letting it fall from her hand to hit the wooden floor with a dull, wet thump. Then with trembling fingers she tried to pin her hair back in place.

The old gentleman threw another log on the fire, making it hiss and spit like an angry cat.

"Got a mirror there on the wall," he said to Cassie, jerking his head toward the spot.

Cassie's eyes followed his nod, and she saw a piece of broken mirror tacked to the rough wall with several small pieces of stick. The surface was yellowed and streaked, and she was sure it wouldn't help much with her task. But to please the old man, she rose from her chair and faced the mirror while she pinned her hair in place as best as she could. The glimpses she could get of her rain-spattered face and sodden hair were not encouraging.

Samuel was soon back, dripping water, but he had brought one of Cassie's bags.

"I thought you might like some dry clothes," he suggested as he lifted the case for her to see. She cast a quick glance around the one small room, but the old man was already reaching for his buckskin coat.

"Got a few chores to do," he said around his pipe. "Might as well git 'em cared fer now. You folk jest make yerselves to home here."

And so saying he tugged at the stubborn door, stepped through into the driving rain, and pulled the door closed behind him.

Cassie reached for the bag. She would lose no time in getting into something more comfortable.

———

They spent the night with the old rancher. There was only one cot and he insisted that Cassie use it. There were no sheets, only two worn and faded Hudson Bay blankets. The pillow had no case and was hard and lumpy, and inwardly she cringed. But Cassie knew better than to complain.

So this was Samuel's West. It was every bit as crude and ugly as any of the stories she had heard. She had no intention of staying in such a desolate and heathen land—none whatever. Surely Samuel could see for himself that she did not belong here. She would not need to force his decision. She was sure he would reach the right one on his own.

————

The sun was shining through the dirty window when she awoke the next morning. She was alone in the room and for one minute panic seized her. Surely the old man had not done something terrible to Samuel.

And then she heard voices outside, drawing near to the cabin.

"An' this here ol' bear's been a-robbin' my calves fer three springs runnin' now. I figure as how this winter I'm gonna find his den and smoke 'im on out iffen it's the last thing I do."

"Be careful," warned Samuel. "You know that a sleeping bear doesn't take kindly to being roused."

"Well, the way I see it—," went on the old fellow, and the voices moved away.

Cassie stretched to take some of the kinks from her limbs. Then she climbed from the bed and looked with disgust at her messy skirts. She had been unable to undress properly for bed the night before. She didn't think it fair to drive the man from his warm fireside out into the rain again. Now she was wrinkled and frazzled and in need of a good hot bath.

But a bath was not to be. There was not even opportunity to change her attire, for the men soon returned and Samuel announced that they were set to be on their way again as soon as they had breakfasted on flapjacks and coffee.

Chapter Ten

Settling In

It didn't take long for Cassie to realize that Samuel had no intention of turning the mare around and heading back toward Calgary to buy a ticket to Montreal.

He seemed especially pleased with the day, the plodding mare, his sturdy buggy, and even the rutted road that no longer kicked up dust in their faces. Cassie felt that the only attraction was found in the mountains to the west.

"I don't think it will get too hot today," Samuel observed, cocking his head to study the morning sky.

Cassie didn't think it was likely either as she clasped her shawl about her, trying desperately to draw warmth from it.

But as the day wore on it did get warm. Cassie eventually discarded her shawl and later longed for some shade.

It took most of the morning to complete the journey, and when they arrived in Jaret, Cassie found it to be just as she had feared. It was a dreary, plain little town, with a few buildings lining a main street of sorts. Wooden sidewalks stretched lazily in front of some of the buildings. The others were reached by trekking through the dust—or the mud—whatever might be in season.

Scattered here and there were the village homes. They were mostly clapboard, many unpainted, a few with little yards hidden behind picket fences.

"My," said Cassie, "it certainly is—unadorned."

Samuel chuckled at her choice of words.

"She is, isn't she?" he admitted, but he seemed delighted with "her."

"You grew up here?" Cassie inquired, finding it difficult to think of anyone raising a family in the area.

"On a farm a few miles east of town."

Cassie lifted her eyes to the east. Bald prairie stretched as far as her eyes could see. She grimaced but made no comment.

"Where are your sisters?"

"They've married and moved away. One is in Vancouver, the other in Edmonton."

Samuel guided the mare down the street and stopped in front of an unpainted frame building. "Why don't you get down and stretch your legs," he invited Cassie. "I need a few things here at the hardware and then we'll go on down to see the house." Excitement tinged his voice.

Cassie knew he was anxious to show her what he had picked for her future home. She climbed from the buggy with the help of his hand, shielding her eyes from the bright summer sun to look down the street and then up. She saw nothing that looked promising. When Samuel turned to enter the hardware, she started off in the direction that seemed to offer the least dust for her skirts.

She didn't walk far. She had taken only a few steps when she remembered the appalling condition of her gown and hair. With a red face she hurried back to the buggy, climbed aboard and pretended to be fully absorbed in the book she had been reading.

Women passed on the street. She felt sure they would have greeted her, but she was totally unprepared to make anyone's acquaintance. She pushed her nose farther into her book and watched them out of the corner of her eye.

Samuel soon returned with many packages piled in his arms. A man with a rather dirty brown apron came with him, carrying a good share of the load.

"Folks will be mighty glad to have you back—mighty glad," the man was saying. "Couldn't believe the good news when you writ thet letter. Everyone fer miles will be jealous of us, havin' our very own doc. Most folks have to travel clear into Calgary—or else Lethbridge. Long journey when they've got a sick one in tow."

Samuel thanked the man for his help and turned to Cassie. "I'd like you to meet my wife, Mr. Stockwood. Cassandra Smith. Cassandra, our hardware owner, Mr. Stockwood."

Cassie flushed with embarrassment but removed the book from her face long enough to properly greet the man.

"Pleased to meet ya, Mrs. Smith. Whole town been buzzin' ever since we heard that Sammie had picked hisself a wife. Mighty glad to bid ya welcome. Mighty glad." And he wiped a huge, rough hand on his stained apron and extended it to her.

Cassie had no choice but to accept the proffered hand. Her small one seemed smothered in the big one. He squeezed firmly and Cassie feared that she might wince, but he released his hold, stepped back and gave her a hearty grin, then moved away so they could proceed.

"I don't expect the team and wagon for several hours yet," said Samuel, "but we can go on down and see the house while we wait."

He clucked to the mare, and the buggy moved down the dusty street. Cassie was glad to escape curious eyes.

They pulled up in front of a small frame home. At one point it had been painted white. Bits of the paint still showed on the boards. There was a fenced yard, but a few of the posts were leaning precariously and some of the pickets lay on the ground instead of sharing their task of protecting the yard from intruders.

There was no walk, simply a trodden path that had mostly given way to weeds and wild grass. There also had been a garden at one time. Cassie could spot the place by the increased growth of weeds in the area.

One windowpane was broken and a rag of curtain dangled in the soft breeze, lifting now and then to wave a feeble greeting and then drop back into place.

The whole thing looked dismal and drab to Cassie, but when she dared to glance toward Samuel, she found him grinning.

"Needs some work," he said simply, "but it seems solid enough. Shouldn't take more than a few days to get it into proper shape."

Then he turned to Cassie, his hazel eyes sparkling with teasing and said softly, "Do you wish to be carried over the threshold now, Mrs. Smith, or do you want me to wait until we are settled?"

Cassie flushed, then tried hard to reply with the same carefree manner, "Well, I believe I will wait until you have finished your husbandly task of repairs," she said lightly.

Samuel grinned, pushed back his lock of wayward hair with one hand and reached for Cassie with the other.

He drew her close against his side and pressed a kiss against her hair.

"It looks like flame in the sunshine," he whispered of her hair. "I think I'll call you Red." His eyes twinkled.

Cassie was grateful he hadn't said "carrots."

"I've arranged for us to stay at Mrs. Clement's while I do the repairs," he surprised her by saying. "I told her we'd be there for dinner so we'd better get going."

Cassie felt relieved. At least they would be given a decent place to stay while Samuel worked on the house. With any measure of good luck, she might never have to move into the little house at all.

But if Cassie had been relieved to hear that they were to share accommodation elsewhere, her pleasure was short-lived when she viewed the new quarters.

It was an old rambling house, tacked and held together with bits of this and pieces of that. It had never known paint, nor had the yard ever been raked or trimmed. One scraggly tree stood near the door, dragging pitiful branches dangerously close to one's head upon entrance. Even Cassie had to duck in order to avoid having the pins torn from her bonnet in passing.

They were welcomed by a reed-thin woman with a sharp chin and sharper eyes. She seemed to look right through Cassie, and the younger woman wondered if the older woman was studying her soul and finding it wanting.

Mrs. Clement clicked loose false teeth when she talked—and she talked often and profusely.

"Expected ya last night. Had the bed all ready," she began, making the words sound almost like an accusation.

"We had hoped to be here but a storm held us up," explained Samuel.

She eyed Cassie sharply, seeming to put all of the blame on her. "Locals woulda jest kept travelin'," she observed.

"It was too hard on the mare to pull the buggy through the mud," said Samuel, and Cassie was pleased that he did not allow her to be held responsible.

"Where'd ya bed?" clicked the woman as she led them down a dark hall and pushed open a creaking door.

"Stayed with a fella by the name of Hank," replied Samuel.

The woman's sharp eyes brightened. "Hank, eh? Never could turn one away, ol' Hank. Take in any stray."

Cassie wasn't sure she liked being called a stray. Particularly in the way that Mrs. Clement had spoken the word, but she made no comment.

Mrs. Clement turned to look at them as she held the door open, her eyes snapping, her teeth clicking. "Heard ya had red hair," she said to Cassandra. "It sure is red all right. Got the temper to go along with it, I 'spect."

Cassie could feel her cheeks beginning to flame. She also felt Samuel's soft touch on her arm. With great difficulty she decided to prove the woman wrong. Her chin came up and her green eyes snapped but she held her tongue.

She passed by the woman through the door and looked at the room that was to be theirs for the next several days.

It was small. Barely big enough for them to pass each other. The bed was small, too, but it took most of the space. Hooks lined the walls, and Cassie knew that they were to suffice for a wardrobe. An old dresser stood against the wall under the single window and on it sat a cracked blue pitcher in a chipped cream bowl. One worn towel hung limply from a peg over the bed. Cassie realized she was seeing her bedroom, bathroom, and parlor all in one brief glance.

"Put fresh water in the pitcher jest a couple hours ago,"

the woman was saying. "You can wash up if you've a mind to. Jest throw the used water out the winda. Dinner will be in ten minutes or so."

And with those words she left.

Cassie did not turn to look at Samuel. She was afraid he might see what she did not wish to reveal. Surely, surely, Samuel would realize now that they couldn't possibly stay in this wilderness town. Surely he would tell her not to bother to unpack her cases, that they would just climb aboard the buggy, flick the reins over the mare and head straight back to Calgary.

But Samuel was not speaking. He crossed the torn linoleum on the floor and leaned to open the window.

"A little breeze would feel good," he said cheerfully as he hoisted the single unit. But not a breath of air stirred the limp flour-sack curtain.

"You go ahead and wash," he invited Cassie, pouring some of the tepid water into the basin.

Cassie washed, then dried on the scant towel. Samuel did not even change the water but proceeded to wash after her, sharing the same towel she had used. Then he did exactly as bidden and leaned from the window to throw the basin of water into the yard beyond.

The dinner was good. Cassie had to admit that. Though it was simple fare, Mrs. Clement was a good cook. But the older woman chattered and clicked and asked candid questions the entire meal. Cassie ate hurriedly, wishing to return to their room—their tiny little room.

"You didn't get much sleep last night," Samuel encouraged her. "Why don't you lie down and have a nap? I'm going over to see where I will start on the house."

Cassie nodded, only too glad to comply.

But the room was stuffy warm. If she opened the window the flies came in, and if she shut the window and killed off the flies, she suffered from the heat.

At last she stretched out, exhausted, and slept in spite of herself. When she awakened it was well into the afternoon. She debated whether to stay where she was and try to read in the intense heat, or to escape the little room and walk down the street to see Samuel.

She moved to the window and looked out on the sultry day. A dust devil twirled a sandy cloud round and round before depositing it on a stretch of broken sidewalk. In the distance the bare plains seemed to dance with the haze of heat waves. A few scraggly chickens scratched fruitlessly in the dust of the path. Cassie turned from it all with a lump in her throat.

"So much for bringing culture," she whispered, fighting back tears that threatened to come. "These people wouldn't understand it. They are more concerned with keeping the dust out of the flour bin."

Cassie went back to bed.

————

"How does one make contact for household help?" Cassie asked their landlady innocently one day while the two of them sat on the back porch sharing a pitcher of lemonade.

The lady looked at her with a puzzled frown. She clicked her teeth once or twice but said nothing.

"Where does one find one's help?" Cassie repeated, thinking that the woman might not have heard or understood her question.

"What ya meanin'?" said Mrs. Clement. "What ya wantin' help fer? Thought yer man had him all the help he needs."

"No. No. I mean for housekeeping. Cooking. For me, after we are settled."

The woman looked at Cassie as though she couldn't possibly be hearing right. "Ya havin' a baby?" she asked candidly.

Cassie flushed. "Of course not," she quickly countered. "We've just recently been married."

"Only folks I know who have house help are the ones sick abed, having new babies where things ain't quite right, or they got 'em too many little ones to handle alone," said Mrs. Clement.

Cassie refused to blush.

"Every woman I know has household help," she said with a hint of defiance.

"Well, it ain't done here," went on Mrs. Clement, her teeth clicking noisily. "Folks would all wonder jest what was wrong with ya."

Cassie did flush then, but before she could make any defense Mrs. Clement spoke again. "Ya don't know how to cook or keep house?" she asked without embarrassment.

"Of course I know," said Cassie with a slight lift of her head. "My mother saw to it that I learned all of the arts of—"

"Then why ain't ya aimin' to do it?" asked the good woman.

Cassie swallowed hard. Her green eyes met the sharp smoky blue eyes of the woman before her. "I will be doing it," she responded almost coolly.

The woman nodded, clicked her teeth, and stood to her feet. "Guess I gotta git those potatoes peeled fer supper," she said, and left Cassie alone on the porch. Cassie never mentioned the idea of household help again—not even to Samuel.

Cassie knew she should be interested in the little house Samuel said was taking shape nicely. She supposed that he expected her to walk the short distance daily to see for herself the progress being made. But for some reason, Cassie could not bring herself to do that.

She found a quiet, almost cool spot behind the house where the breeze sometimes teased her hair and the sun did not beat down with the same vigor. There she busied herself with hemming new curtains from some material she had brought along. Her excuse seemed to be sufficient to keep prying eyes and wagging tongues from condemning the new bride.

For several days she saw Samuel only at mealtime and at the end of long, busy days when he was almost too tired from his labors to even bring her up-to-date on his doings. Anxious to be in their new quarters, he had hired some help, and from the pounding that Cassie heard as she hid herself away on the sagging back porch, it seemed indeed that progress must be taking place.

Then one day as Cassie stitched her last curtain hem, a grinning Samuel appeared and announced joyfully that the little house was ready for occupancy. Cassie braced herself for the worst and allowed her things to be loaded in the buggy. Then she stepped up, Samuel's arm giving her aid, and sat stiffly aboard while the little mare bore them down the dusty street to their first home.

Cassie was unprepared for the change of its appearance. The fence had been mended and the walk cleared. The white painted exterior had been restored, the windows fixed and the tattered curtain gone from view. Proudly Samuel helped her from the buggy, then whisked her up into his arms and carried her across the threshold as he had promised. Cassie could feel the tears forming droplets in her eyes. She didn't know why she was crying. She only knew that something deep within her was responding in some way to the man whom she loved.

He placed her on her feet and grinned broadly. "Our parlor," he said with a wave of his hand.

Cassie looked about her at the simple furniture. Two rockers sat before the fireplace and a sofa covered with a bright quilt graced the far wall. In the background a bureau stood, new and unscarred, before a staid white-painted wall. No rugs, no curtains, no pictures yet softened the bareness. Cassie let her glance slide over everything Samuel had provided, and suddenly the woman in her flamed into life. She had a house. Simple—yet clean. She would make it into a home for Samuel. Not elegant—not even pretty—but a home nonetheless. She turned to her husband and wrapped her arms about his neck. "Thank you," she choked out, unable to say more.

But even then her inner being whispered, "I'm sure I can be fine here—until you decide it's time to move back to Montreal."

Chapter Eleven

Adjustments

Cassie quickly busied herself with adding "touches" to their little frame home while Samuel set up his practice and became too busy almost at once. On some days, Cassie felt as if she had been deserted. Samuel was gone from daybreak to past sundown, and after her daily chores had been completed, there was really nothing for her to do.

She refused to sit idly on her back porch, but finding enough to fill the hours of the day was difficult. She knew no one of her own age with similar interests and, worst of all, Samuel still had not breathed one word about returning to the East.

The townsfolk had been friendly enough, but Cassie felt a bit strange with them. Unconsciously she held herself apart, feeling that they could not possibly understand her background, her breeding—thus, her thoughts and feelings.

One day as she went to the store for a few items, she happened to pass a cluster of women. They were unaware of her presence until she was well within earshot.

"She's a bit high-hat," she heard Mrs. Clement click. "But the West will take thet outta her quick enough."

Cassie bit her lip and hurried on. But she knew the woman had been speaking of her—and another wall was built.

So Cassie stayed at home in her own little kitchen as much as she could. And even though she detested household chores of any sort, she soon learned that they were one way she could pass the time.

She grew more and more lonely and did not know where to turn for friendship. She had to get out. She had to. Yet where could she go? What could she do?

One morning as she strolled past the little community church, the thought came to her that maybe here she could find something to do. Without a pause, she turned up the walk to the parsonage.

"Oh my dear," said the kind elderly wife of the pastor. "We do need help—in so many areas. What would you be interested in doing?"

Cassie hardly knew. She had attended church all her life, but she had never really been involved in any active role. She had left the many tasks to others.

"I—I'm not sure," she responded with a flush. "Do—do you have any suggestions?"

"Well, we do need a teacher for the children."

"I—I have never taught, but I—I guess I could try."

"Wonderful!" the good woman beamed. "I'm sure that Mrs. Wilma Canterbury would be glad to give you suggestions. She has been teaching a class, but with the new twins . . ." She let her voice trail off, but Cassie was able to complete the thought on her own.

"I don't suppose you know how to read music?" the woman went on rather hesitantly.

Cassie nodded her head. "I have had many years of lessons," she admitted.

At that the lady really beamed. "Oh, my husband will be so pleased," she enthused. "We don't have an organist."

"But I only play the piano," Cassie was quick to explain.

"Organ. Piano. No difference." The woman was determined. "They both have keys."

"But there is a difference." Cassie was sure. "The organ has pipes and foot pedals and—"

"Not our organ," the woman said, shaking her head. "It just has pedals and you pump."

"Oh my," said Cassie, wondering what she might have

gotten herself into. "I'm not sure I can do that."

"Well, you can practice as much as you like. The church is always open," Mrs. Ray said, seeming to feel that the issue had been nicely cared for.

Cassie nodded mutely and was about to take her leave when the older woman added, "Are you coming to the Sewing Circle on Thursday?"

"I—I don't remember hearing about it," Cassie responded.

"We have it here—every first Thursday of the month. We meet at one o'clock and we need all the hands we can get."

Cassie nodded. She felt quite confident of her needle skills, thanks to her mother's insistence.

"Of course we don't just sew," the woman went on. "We have a prayer time and a missions study—and we do a bit of neighborly visitin' too," she admitted with a smile.

Cassie's eyes suddenly brightened. She was so lonely and so bored. A visit with neighborhood ladies sounded like a wonderful idea.

"I'll be there," she said, a hint of enthusiasm in her voice.

That night she could hardly wait to tell Samuel about her day's adventure and of how she would be practicing the little pump organ at the church and teaching the children under the tutorage of Wilma Canterbury and meeting to sew and visit with the missions ladies. But as she waited for him so she could dish the simple supper meal, Bobby Adams ran up her walk to rap loudly on the door.

In his hand he held a bright shiny nickel and he studied it carefully as he spoke to her.

"Doc Smith asked me to run over an' tell ya he can't get home yet. He jest got called outta town to doctor somebody thet got his leg caught or somethin'," said the boy, his eyes constantly on his nickel.

"When will Dr. Smith be home?" asked Cassie, disappointment welling up and showing in her eyes and voice.

"I dunno. He didn't say. Oh, yeah. He said don't hold supper, he'll likely be late. Thet's all he said."

The boy looked anxious to be off to spend his nickel, so

Cassie thanked him and let him go.

She couldn't eat the supper. The few bites she took kept sticking in her throat, so she finally gave up, cleared the table, and looked for something to read. There was nothing new, and she had read her treasured books so many times over that she couldn't keep her mind on them. She wished she could go for a long walk in the cool of the evening, but it was another thing that simply wasn't done around here. She knew no one to visit. There was no play, no opera, no anything. Cassie went early to bed and cried herself to sleep—again.

She didn't hear Samuel slip quietly into bed very late. During their hurried breakfast the next morning, Cassie tried to tell him about her new activities, but somehow the glow of it was gone, though Samuel was interested and approving.

After Cassie had finished her household duties, she slipped on a bonnet and hurried off to the little church at the edge of town. At first she felt self-conscious about opening the door and walking across the plain board floor to the little organ.

Carefully and almost stealthily she lifted the lid to expose the keyboard, then let her fingers tentatively press down a key.

Nothing happened.

She extended her hand a little more aggressively and tried another key with a bit more force. Still nothing happened. Suddenly Cassie remembered that she was not dealing with a piano but a pump organ. There would be no sound until she provided some air for the bellows.

She reached down and ran a hand over the worn bench to check it for dust. It wasn't too bad, though it was dusty. She swished her hand back and forth in hopes of removing most of the problem and then settled herself on the bench, carefully arranging her skirts, and felt for the pedals with her foot.

There were no pedals.

Puzzled, she stood again and began to peer around this way and that. After some time she discovered a little door at the lower front of the organ. But the door had no handle that Cassie could see.

She was about to give up and go home when the church door opened, spilling bright sunshine across the plain wooden floor. It startled Cassie and a little gasp escaped her.

"S'cuse me, my dear," said a kindly voice Cassie recognized as that of the gentle old pastor. "I didn't mean to frighten you. Mrs. Ray said you had agreed to play the organ for us, and when we saw you coming to the church she sent me on out to make sure you had the hymnbook. We've only got one with the music. Rest of the folks just use the words."

Cassie looked around. She could see no hymnbook.

"It's there—in the organ bench," the pastor explained. "Can't tell you how thankful we are to have someone who can play. You just go ahead and practice all you've a mind to. Here's a list of the hymns we'll sing on Sunday—unless someone requests a favorite."

Cassie took the lengthy list with trembling fingers.

"We like to sing," the pastor told her. "Only bright spot in a difficult week for some of the people."

Cassie nodded.

"It will make the singing so much more enjoyable for folks. Can't thank you enough for playing for us. And now I'd best leave you alone and let you do your practicing." The pastor turned and was almost to the door before Cassie could get up the courage to call after him.

"Pastor Ray!"

He turned.

With some embarrassment Cassie managed to tell him, "I—I've never played an organ before."

"So Mrs. Ray said. But that's fine. You'll do just fine if you know the notes for a piano. It's the same—"

Cassie interrupted with eyes lowered, "Could—could you

show me how to find the—the bellow pedals, please."

With a chuckle the good man came back and showed Cassie how to lift up the little door and drop the foot pedals into position; then he chuckled softly again and left her on her own.

———

Cassie made a good attempt of accompanying the congregational singing the next Sunday. She flushed a few times over her errors, but the people did not seem to notice. They sang heartily and Cassie wondered if they even heard her mistakes.

Samuel seemed tremendously proud of her, and that made Cassie feel good. He had been pleased to learn that she would be joining the ladies of the Mission Circle and helping with the Sunday school class.

"It seems my little wife is becoming one of the church pillars," he teased, and in spite of her remonstrance, Cassie had to smile.

But inwardly she answered, *There seems to be no choice. I have no other way to fill my dreary days while you linger on in this little spot at the edge of the world.*

Had Cassie felt free to do so, she would have spoken the words aloud to her young husband, but she did not wish to sow discord. Their brief times together were too precious to spoil with quarrels. Besides, she hoped daily that he would soon be suggesting they return to the comforts and possibilities of the city. Didn't city folk need doctors too?

———

As the weeks marched slowly by with lumbering steps, Cassie watched and waited for each letter from home or from Abigail. When one did arrive she grasped it as her lifeline, read it over and over, and then spent the next hours crying because of her intense loneliness for those she had left behind.

The letters were no comfort to her. They were a constant pain. Either she was waiting with impatience for one to arrive or else she was grieving because one had. And between yearning and sorrowing, Cassandra allowed herself no peace.

When fall came, the leaves on the few small trees that the little town possessed turned gold and left the shelter of the branches to dance freely on the prairie winds. The hot days slowly cooled to bearable, and then one morning as Cassie crossed to the little church for her daily practice, she could feel a definite sting in the morning wind.

"I do believe we are heading for winter," she said to herself, raising her eyes to study the mountains on the horizon.

Sure enough, there on the slopes lay the whiteness of winter snow.

"Oh dear," breathed Cassie. "I had so hoped we would be back East before winter settled in. Perhaps we will get snowbound here until spring."

She hastened her steps as though that would help Samuel more quickly make the long-awaited decision to return East.

She did not spend as long playing the organ that morning. The little building's stove was not in operation yet and her fingers soon became numb with the cold. She hurried home and built up her own fire in the kitchen stove. She felt the need to warm her thoughts as well as thaw her bones.

Tears stung her eyes as she stood at the kitchen window looking out across the expanse of dry prairie grasses that bowed and lifted in the wind. "We are stuck here," she whispered. "I just know we will be stuck here. We won't be able to go home now until spring."

She let the tears run down her cheeks and fall heedlessly to the front of her gown. "What ever will I do?" she cried. "How will I ever manage to survive a prairie winter shut away here in this little house with the wind howling around the corners and Samuel always away on call? I will never make it. I just know I won't. I don't think that he has any—

any idea of how difficult—" And Cassie put her hands over her face and wept for the comfort of her mother and home.

———

It was another three weeks before the first flakes of snow began to drift around the little town, burying the bare brownness of the yards and garden spots. By then Cassie was resigned to staying where she was, but she still hated the thought. Deep down inside a new storm was brewing. She was a bit angry with Samuel. Her anger swung from hurt to frustration to bitterness, and the enemy of her soul used all three to feed her loneliness and dissatisfaction.

"I can't do a thing about it now," she told herself, "but come spring, I am going home."

Samuel must have noticed the difference in his young bride. Or he most certainly would have if his busy practice had given him time to notice anything. But he continued on in the same manner, enthusiastically leaving the house early each morning and whistling his way home again at the end of a long, yet rewarding day. On Sundays he tried to free the day the best he could so he might attend the morning worship service and then share the rest of the time with Cassie. It was the only day that Cassie felt as if she had a husband— and even then it was often interrupted by some emergency.

Cassie planned over and over to use one of those Sundays to tell Samuel exactly how she felt about his West, but his never-changing cheerfulness always made her feel like a whiner, and she couldn't get the words through her choked throat.

"There's no use telling him right now," she would reprimand herself. "We have a whole winter to face with only each other as company. It will be even more difficult if we quarrel. But come spring—come spring I'll ask Samuel to take me home," she determined, breaking the covenant she had made with herself not to force Samuel's hand but to wait until he realized that the West was an impossible place to live. Now he seemed to be so wrapped up in his work that he was blind to everything else, she decided. She knew that if her situation was to change, she would have to demand a release from the horrors of the little town.

"I just can't bear it any longer," she cried almost every day. "I just can't."

Cassie braced herself for a long winter. Somehow she must endure until spring.

To all appearances things remained the same. Each Sunday morning she still taught the children of Jesus' love and God's goodness, then dutifully, even with some pleasure, played for the congregation. On the first Thursday of the month, she met with the Mission Circle at the Rays' and stitched little garments for overseas babies or quilts for needy families, but inwardly her heart was crying out for the winter to end quickly so spring might release her from this prairie prison.

And Samuel had no idea.

———————

Cassie found more to keep her busy with Christmas approaching. She helped bake for the food baskets to be sent to poor families in the city with the Rev. and Mrs. Ray, who would spend their holiday with family in Calgary. She sewed simple garments for a family who had lost their home in a fire. She volunteered for the Christmas program committee and rehearsed with the children every day after school. But none of her frantic activity eased the pain in her heart.

Christmas came and went and she felt first anguish, then relief. She had always loved Christmas. Christmas had meant home and parties and plays and "occasions." There was none of that for her this year. She had feared she would never make it through Christmas in the town of Jaret—Christmas in her own lonely little house. Then it was over—her first Christmas away from home. Surely a bit of her pain would also subside. Besides, now they were on the down side of the long winter. Now she could begin to count the days until spring—and home.

But in March, Cassie discovered she was expecting their first child. The excitement was tempered with disappointment. It would not be wise to travel come spring. She would need to wait until the baby had been safely delivered. But the baby was not due until the first week of October. By the time she could travel they would be heading into a new winter. Would Samuel agree then to her and the new baby traveling the roads to Calgary to catch the train to Montreal?

Chapter Twelve

Beginnings

The weather was quite favorable on the first Thursday of April as Cassie picked her way through the spring mud to the home of Mrs. Ray. She was looking forward to the afternoon. The ladies of the small group were no longer just names and faces, and though she didn't feel that she had much in common with any of them, at least they were company.

The usual group lined the small parlor, sewing in their laps and needles in their hands. But as Cassie let her eyes scan the room, and greeted familiar neighbors, she noted that a new face had joined the crowd. Something about that face drew her. It wasn't just that the young woman seemed to be about her age. And it wasn't just that she noticed almost instantly that the woman was expecting. There was something else in the face that seemed to pull at Cassie.

As the meeting began, Cassie found herself lifting her eyes to catch glimpses of the woman. Where had she come from and would she be staying? But Mrs. Ray was soon to answer both questions.

"Ladies," the pastor's wife said, "we are most happy to welcome a new member of the Sewing Circle today. Mrs. Foigt grew up in Winnipeg. She and her husband have purchased the town drugstore and will be joining our little congregation. We are so happy to have them here.

"Mrs. Foigt has some interesting experiences that perhaps she can share with us sometime, for they have lived in the North before coming here. Perhaps at one of our meetings we can have her tell us a little of life near the Arctic."

Cassie could not keep her eyes off the face of the young woman. What was it about her?

Mrs. Clement's voice interrupted Cassie's thoughts. "What's wrong with now? We can listen and sew at the same time," she said bluntly.

"Well, it seems rather short notice," responded Mrs. Ray with a little chuckle. "It may be that Mrs. Foigt would prefer a bit of time to sort of get acquainted and—" She stopped and looked inquiringly at the newcomer.

"I wouldn't mind," said the young woman softly. "I—I haven't prepared anything, but if you'd just ask questions, I'd be glad to answer them."

"Thank you," Mrs. Ray replied sincerely. "Perhaps you could begin by telling us where you were and why you were there."

The young woman stood to her feet. She seemed a bit timid, but there was a serenity about her that put everyone at ease.

That's it! thought Cassie. *She seems so—so totally—calm. At peace.* But the young woman was speaking.

"I went North because my husband went North," she said and smiled. "Actually, my husband had a dream of one day owning his own drugstore—but by the time he paid for his education, he had little money to make a purchase. A friend visited and told us that if a man had a few good years in the North, he could make a lot of money trapping and selling furs. I didn't like the idea of trapping. I don't think my husband did either—but he did want the store and he didn't know of another way to make enough money to purchase one.

"So we talked about it and finally decided that it was what we should do. We moved up there shortly after we were married three years ago. We didn't make lots of money—but we did make enough to come back and put a down payment on the little drugstore here in this town."

She hesitated as though awaiting her first question. It came quickly.

"What was it like?"

She smiled then. A soft, gentle smile. "It was cold and white and barren," she replied. "I thought I would never warm up. Everything one did had to be done enshrouded in furs. Even the cabin was cold, though we kept the fire burning at all times."

"Were ya by yerself or in a town?"

"We were in a village. Mostly made up of native people."

"Were they—did you visit back and forth?"

"There wasn't a lot of visiting. Most of one's time in the North is spent keeping a fire going and looking after one's needs. In the beginning I didn't know anybody. Most of the people couldn't speak English and I couldn't speak the native language, so it was hard at first to really make friends. We'd smile and nod when we met—but that was about all."

Silence. Each of the eleven women in the room seemed to be considering the situation.

"Weren't there any whites?" asked a frail elderly woman tucked away in a corner of the room.

"A few other trappers lived there, but only one of them had a white wife and she was quite old and not well. We did have a Mountie, but he was single and was usually on the trail. I didn't get to know him well, though my husband did. He liked him."

"What was the village like?"

"There was one store—a trading post. You couldn't find much there but you could get essentials. They carried more traps and knives than they did grocery items." She smiled again as though she found that amusing. Cassie cringed at the thought.

"The village was scattered little shacks, I guess," she said with a careless shrug.

"Wasn't that—sorta hard?" asked Mrs. Trent, her eyes wide.

She must feel as I do, Cassie was thinking. *I can't think of anything more horrid than living in an old shack with everyone around me speaking a different language—and in constant winter.*

But Mrs. Foigt was continuing. "It was. At first, I—I guess I thought I'd never be able to stand it for one year— let alone three or four. We didn't know how many years it might take. But then God began to work in my heart. I knew He had promised, 'I will be with thee whithersoever thou goest,' and I knew that must also include the North. I had told my husband I would support him in what he was planning to do, and I decided that if I was going to do that and not become ill from tension, or bitter from resentment, then I had to work on my attitude.

"Well, I did try to work on it. The harder I tried to accept things, the angrier I became inside and the more I hated the North. I finally decided I could either let my anger and bitterness make me—and Morris—totally miserable for three or four years—or I could go to God for the help I needed. I knew I couldn't do it by myself. I had to learn to give the whole thing over to Him. When I learned to be totally honest and open with God, He was able to give me the help I asked Him for. The years in the North turned out to be good years.

"Oh, I don't say they were easy years—but they were growing years—and they were good years for Morris and me. We learned to love each other even more, and we both learned that the same—the same commitment we made to God and to each other to get us through those difficult times also can see us through whatever life brings to us. We know that just because we are back home, to a lovely little town, with all the fine things of life and a church and new friends and a nice little house where we can keep warm even in the winter—that doesn't mean that things will always go easy for us. Difficult things can take one by surprise wherever one lives."

She seemed so sure of her words. Cassie was having a hard time keeping up with her own thoughts. This young woman was describing their town, their simple little back-of-the-world prairie town as "lovely," "with fine things." At first Cassie felt a surge of pity that the girl knew so little about real life. Real living. Then just as quickly she felt shame. Was she justified in feeling as she did? Certainly this prairie town was far from the culture and refinement of Montreal, but she was not suffering any real physical hardships.

Then Mrs. Clement with her usual candor asked frankly, "This yer first baby?"

The serene eyes shadowed for just a moment, then the same look of peace returned. "No," she said softly. "We buried our first son in the North."

Cassie felt her whole being tremble.

How can you? How can you? she wished to cry out. *You stand there and—and say that just as though—just as though—*

But the woman was speaking again. "That was when I really learned to love my neighbors," she said softly, and Cassie thought she saw tears glistening in her eyes. "When our baby was sick the native women made sure that I was never alone. Morris was out on the trapline, and there was no way to get word to him. We didn't have medicine—but the women—they were with me—night and day. We tried some of the native remedies but nothing would work. But they didn't leave me. They brought food, they tended my fire, they just sat silently beside me. Then I knew—I really knew that there was a God and that He loved me. That He cared about my loneliness and my sick baby. That He sent His ministering angels to care for me—way up in that frozen northland—and I knew I could trust Him."

"But yer baby died," clicked Mrs. Clement in reminder.

"Yes. Yes, he did. God took him home. It wasn't what I would have wanted but—God did it so gently. And every woman in the village knew exactly what I was going through. There's not a mother up there who hasn't lost at least one child. If I had been here—in some town or city—I would never have received the love, the support, the understanding that I received from those who knew exactly how I was suffering. And they showed their love in a hundred different ways. You see, by the time I left I had a bit of their language—and many wonderful friends."

A tear slid unheeded down her cheek, but she lifted a smiling face and said in confident manner, "I have learned, firsthand, that God is great and God is good. I thank Him with all my heart for my years in the North—my years of learning to totally depend upon Him."

She smiled again and sat down quietly.

The hands holding the needles had forgotten to sew. Cassie was vaguely aware that many of them reached for hankies instead. Noses blew. Bodies shifted in their chairs. Throats were cleared. But for Cassie there was still confusion. *What did she mean?* How could she have gone through what she had and stand before them smiling? *I need to think about this,* she told herself. *I need plenty of time to sort it out before I understand it. Before I—accept or reject it.*

And Cassie was the first in the circle to turn her attention back to her sewing.

———

Cassie did a great deal of thinking and mental sorting over the next few days. She still didn't fully understand all that the new neighbor had tried to share, but she did come to some conclusions.

First of all, she decided that the young woman knew God in a way she herself did not. Cassie had been faithful in church attendance. Her parents had seen to that. She had known the Bible stories better than any other child in the catechism classes. She had more prizes for memorization, perfect attendance and Bible knowledge than she knew what to do with—but she didn't know God the way this Mrs. Foigt did.

But neither could she really understand what God had to do with one's acceptance of a situation. Her unhappiness was not because she felt that God had deserted her. After all, she was busily engaged in the local church. It seemed safe to assume that God was also there. No, she was unhappy because she didn't care for this rough, unpolished way of life. She didn't have her mother, she didn't have Abigail. She didn't have her own room with its chintz-covered window seat and carpeted floors. She didn't like the West. But she did love Samuel. At least most of the time she was quite sure she still loved Samuel.

Cassie continued to wrestle with her problem and then came to one conclusion. She would try to get to know young Mrs. Foigt better. Maybe by watching her closely, she would discover what it was about the woman that gave her such an aura of peace.

Chapter Thirteen

Friendship

It was not difficult to become acquainted with Mrs. Foigt. The town was small, the atmosphere open and friendly, the town druggist and the town doctor worked closely together, and they saw the Foigts in church every Sunday. Besides this, Cassie felt drawn to the young woman and could sense from her response that it was mutual.

And as an added measure for common ground, both young women were expecting a child.

It wasn't long until they were finding little excuses to pop over to each other's houses and stay for a cup of tea and a chat.

"How are you feeling?" Mrs. Foigt asked one morning when she noticed that the teacup sat before Cassie almost untouched.

Cassie smiled but pushed the cup a bit farther from her.

"Quite well. But some mornings—I just can't even think of trying to swallow something."

"I know what you mean. I had so much morning sickness with our first baby. And all I had to eat was—" She stopped and screwed up her face as though the very thought made her feel ill now. "Wild meat and pan-fried breads. I didn't enjoy the fare at the best of times, but then—" She shuddered and Cassie shuddered with her.

"I don't know how you ever stood it!" Cassie exclaimed. "I would never have been able to do it. I mean—the whole experience. Of being there in the cold with no one as a close friend and your husband always out on the trapline. I couldn't have done it."

Mrs. Foigt smiled and toyed with her china cup. "It really wasn't so bad—after I gave in," she answered softly. "It was fighting my circumstances that gave me pain."

"But, Mrs. Foigt—" began Cassie.

"Please. Please, can we be less formal? I would love it if you would call me Virginia."

Cassie nodded her red head. "I'd like that," she responded. "And my name is—" She hesitated for a brief instance and then made a quick decision. It was time to do some growing up. "My name is Cassandra," she went on.

"Cassandra. What a pretty name."

"I thought the same of Virginia," Cassandra returned, then went on. "I've really wanted to talk with you—well, very personally. I—I feel that you have—well, that you have something—a peace or something I don't have. I know you've—well, had to—what would you say—reach out for God through your difficult experience. But—well, I guess what I really want to know is—how you did it. I mean—"

But Virginia was smiling. She seemed to understand Cassandra's questioning heart more than her halting words.

"It didn't happen instantly. I mean, the initial contact, the reaching out to God and knowing that He was there— that He was waiting and anxious to—to be God—that happened perhaps in—well, an experience of faith. But the rest—it was a case of growing and learning and committing as He showed me new things." She hesitated just a moment. "And prayer—much prayer," she added.

"I—I pray," Cassandra tried to explain. "I mean—I was taught to pray. But it seemed—it seems He doesn't pay much attention to my prayers. Why does He answer yours—and not mine?"

Cassandra let her gaze fall to the pattern of the table-cloth. She still wasn't sure how to phrase her questions.

"Do you know God?" asked Virginia gently.

"I've been brought up in the church. I've always known there is a God. I—"

"But do you know *Him?*" repeated Virginia, just as softly, but with emphasis.

Cassandra nodded her head. "I—I think I do," she answered as honestly as she knew how.

"If you just think you do, you maybe don't really know Him," said Virginia, "just about Him."

Cassandra lifted her head and looked into the clear blue eyes before her. "I—I don't think I understand," she said, shaking her head. "I—I really don't see a difference."

"Do you believe that the king of England exists?"

"Why, yes. Of course. Everyone knows he does."

"You are sure that he exists, which of course he does. Do you know him?"

Cassandra laughed a little laugh at Virginia's game. "Of course not," she said, "I've never had the privilege."

"That's really too bad," said Virginia with a grin. "I hear he has untold wealth that he could bestow if he had a mind to—wealth that will undoubtedly be left as a legacy to his family."

They chuckled together; then Virginia continued. "Well, I think it is much the same with God. Many believe that He exists—and well they should. The evidence is all around us. But they don't know Him. They have never had a—a personal friendship with Him established. They've never become a part of His family."

Cassandra's frown deepened.

"We can't grow—we can't lean on Him—we can't find His peace until we know Him himself. That is the starting point. Once we are a part of His family, we get to draw on the benefits. Do you see?"

"I—I think I'm beginning to understand what you are saying. But—but, how does one—how does one—get in?" asked Cassandra lamely.

"By realizing that He is more than our God. He is our Savior. We need to admit that we aren't fit to be a part of the family because of our sinfulness. Then we accept the fact that He has done something on our behalf to care for that great need."

"You mean Christ's death?"

"Yes, His death. In substitute for us. He took our place."

"I taught that lesson to the Sunday school class just last Sunday," admitted Cassandra. And in defense she continued. "And I believed what I was teaching. I wasn't being a hypocrite."

"Of course not. But did you—did you apply it to Cassandra Smith? Did you feel a great surge of—of thankfulness that He had done that for you? Did your heart nearly burst with the joy of knowing that because He died, you could stand before God with a clean record—and heart? You will not need to face the embarrassment—the penalty—of judgment."

Virginia's eyes were shining. Her cheeks were aglow with the marvel of the forgiveness of which she spoke. Cassandra looked at the beauty of the radiant face before her and shook her head slowly.

"No," she said in almost a whisper. "No, I didn't. I really didn't feel a thing. I—I just repeated facts that I've known from childhood."

"Then tell Him," said Virginia. "Bow before Him and claim His great pardon. Let Him know that you want to be His child—that you accept His—His gift of—of infinite measure. Thank Him for His unconditional love and—and accept His conditional forgiveness."

"Conditional?"

"Conditional on only one thing—your *receiving* of it."

At the question in Cassandra's eyes, Virginia went on. "Believe! Repent! That's what He has asked of us. When we meet those conditions—we become His—a part of His family—then—then we have our base for growing in Him. We are the branches—drawing strength and nourishment from the Vine. Then we have the right and privilege of drawing on His resources. Once we really know Him—we are heirs to all of His heavenly treasures—and—and He is so rich—so rich with all good things. Even more than the king of England." She smiled, then added, "Love, joy, peace, patience, goodness. Oh, so much. He wants to shower good gifts upon His children."

Cassandra leaned back in her chair and studied the face before her. She shook her head slowly. She had heard preaching all her life—but she had never heard a sermon like the one her new friend just delivered. There was something about Virginia, a fervor that assured Cassandra the young woman knew intimately that of which she spoke.

Cassandra nodded her head slowly. Restlessly she reached to gather the teacups. She had a lot of thinking to do. A lot of praying. Maybe Virginia was right.

———

"Did you know that one can know God—personally?" she tentatively asked Samuel as they prepared for bed that evening.

Samuel's head came up and he lifted a hand to brush back the straying lock of brown hair.

"You didn't?" he said in disbelief.

Cassandra felt her cheeks grow warm. "I—I thought I did," she managed to respond, "but today I discovered—that I didn't. I really only—only knew about Him. I—I wasn't really—one of the family," she finished lamely.

Samuel did not accuse or argue. He looked at her evenly, willing her to go on and share her heart.

"Virginia and I had a chat," she continued. "She—she helped me to see the difference."

Samuel nodded.

Tears began to form in Cassandra's eyes in spite of her resolve not to shed them. Samuel moved quickly and took her into his arms. She wept in silence for a few minutes before she could continue.

"I am now," she informed him. "A member of the family, I mean. It—it really does make a difference. I—I think that I will teach the children—well—differently now."

Samuel continued to hold her, running his hand up and down the small of her back. Now and then the hand lifted to pat her shoulder.

When he felt that she had finished speaking—and weeping—he leaned to kiss her hair, then her cheek. "I'm glad, my little Red," he whispered against her ear. "I'm so glad. I—I should have realized—as the spiritual head of the home—I should have shared more about my relationship with Him. I'm so glad that Mrs. Foigt was sensitive enough to . . ." He let his voice trail off and kissed her again.

But Cassandra had more tears, this time of joy. "Oh, Samuel," she said with happiness radiating from her tear-streaked face, "it couldn't have happened at a better time. Our baby will have a mother who knows the difference. Now I can teach her the truth."

"Him," laughed Samuel and drew her closer.

Not all Cassandra's lessons in spiritual growth were learned easily, but it did help her to know that she could draw strength and help from beyond herself.

She still disliked the dust and dryness of the little town. She still became frustrated and edgy when Samuel spent hours of his evenings and Sundays with patients rather than with her. She still found the frank tongue of Mrs. Clement difficult to accept. And her temperament, the one that she received along with her red hair, did not change—only altered.

"I wish I wasn't so quick to respond," she said to Samuel one day as she put down her groceries and reached to remove her bonnet.

He lifted his eyes from the paper he was scanning. He had just finished spending the night with a patient and had come home midmorning for a cup of coffee and a breather.

"Mrs. Clement met me in the store and said I looked like I was expecting twins. Right out. Right in front of other customers and—and Mr. Willis."

Cassandra felt her temper rising again at the very thought. She saw Samuel's eyes drop to her growing body. He smiled softly.

"Well, you needn't smirk," cut in Cassandra angrily. "It

doesn't please me to—to look like a—like a walking pork barrel."

Samuel's smile widened in spite of his effort to hide it. He pulled the paper up a bit higher in hopes of concealing his humor.

Cassandra was silent for several minutes as she rather noisily deposited her grocery items in the kitchen cupboards.

When the last item had been put away, she drew a cup from the cupboard, poured herself some of Samuel's coffee and eased her heavy frame onto a kitchen chair.

"I hate looking this way," she said before she took her first sip. "And when someone makes—makes bold mention of it—right in public—well—it—it made me very angry."

Samuel laid aside his paper and reached for her hand.

"So you are wishing God had used a stork, after all?" he said gently.

Cassandra sighed deeply, nodded her head, and then managed a little smile. "It would have been nice," she admitted.

They sat in silence for a moment, each deep in thought, each drawing warmth from the coffee.

"So—," asked Samuel at last, "did you embarrass yourself with a come-back?"

It was a frank, honest question.

Cassandra sighed again. "I—I almost did. I would have," she admitted. "I started to speak. I was—was really going to give Mrs. Clement a piece of my mind, but—but Virginia entered the store—at just that moment and she—she heard. I think she sensed my inner feelings and how near I was to lashing out. Maybe she saw my red face and knew of my anger. I don't know. But she looked at me. Just looked at me and she smiled and gave me just a tiny little nod—like she understood perfectly and I—I bit my tongue. Then she walked straight over and stood beside me and she—she looked even bigger than I did—and she—she didn't seem to be the least embarrassed about it. And she said as sweetly as you can imagine, 'Wouldn't it be grand if we both had twins?' and she smiled right at Mrs. Clement."

Samuel could not hold back a chuckle.

"We walked home together and I—I told her what I thought of Mrs. Clement and her crude tongue. By then we could laugh about it. A little. But I still was angry."

"I'm sure that Mrs. Clement didn't mean—"

"That's what Virginia said. She said, 'She's not mean, Cassandra—just—brutally frank,' and we had a good laugh about that as well."

Samuel patted her hand. "Well, I've got to get back to the office," he said, rising from his chair. "The patients will be stacked up three deep if I don't."

"You look tired," noticed Cassandra, her concern switching to her husband. "You've got to get some sleep, Samuel. You've been working day and night. You can't do that for long. You'll wear yourself out."

He leaned to kiss her. "I'll try to get home early tonight," he promised and reached for his hat and black bag.

When another letter arrived from Abigail, a wave of homesickness washed over Cassandra as she slit the envelope and looked down on the familiar script.

From the very opening line the letter bubbled—just as Abigail had always done.

"I am going to be married," and Cassandra could almost hear her say the words. Shriek the words would have been a more apt description.

"He is wonderful. No, he is not an attorney, and yes, Father was not too happy at first. But Mother worked on him until he gave us his consent, if not his blessing.

"He is a reporter for the local paper and such a dashing, wonderful, exciting person. I still can't believe that he picked me. He must have had the choice of dozens of girls."

And on and on went Abigail's letter.

"I do wish you could be my matron-of-honor. Is it at all possible that you could come?"

Cassandra looked down at her growing front and chuckled softly, but inwardly her heart ached to be able to go home to see Abigail, to see her family, to experience some of the pleasures of her past. Tears made it difficult for her to finish the letter. When she was done she folded it carefully and placed it back in the envelope. Then she reached for her bonnet. She needed a chat with Virginia. She needed someone who understood her, to share in a few minutes of prayer.

———

"Virginia is in labor." Samuel said the words with total calmness as he leaned through the back door and spoke to Cassandra, who stood at the stove preparing the evening meal. "I may not make it home for supper," he continued.

But Cassandra had wheeled around to face him, her eyes big, her face drained of color. Virginia was in labor. Virginia was about to have her baby. Cassandra still had three months to go. Now she would be pregnant all alone.

"Is—is everything all right?" she finally managed to stammer.

"As far as I know. Morris just came to fetch me. I'm going over now. I'll let you know if I get the chance."

He closed the door and Cassandra turned back to the stove to remove another meal that would not be eaten.

The door opened again and she heard Samuel's voice. "Do you want to come?" he asked her.

Cassandra had conflicting thoughts. She would love to go to Virginia. With all her heart she wanted to reassure her friend. On the other hand, she had always hated sickness, pain of any sort, and the sight of blood almost put her on the floor. She paled. "I think I'd better not," she responded and Samuel nodded and closed the door again.

But it was a long evening for Cassandra. She tried to do needlework, tried to read, tried to pray, but her attention span was short. She paced the kitchen, paced the front veranda, paced her bedroom where the small trunk rested that was gradually filling with new baby things.

She twisted her wedding band, wrung her hands, and worried the fringe of her light shawl. But the long hours crawled on and on.

"Oh, why doesn't he come home?" she fretted. "Or at least send word?"

Darkness fell. She knew she should be in bed, but she also knew that she wouldn't sleep. At last her agitation drew her from the house. Clasping the shawl tightly about her shoulders, she set off down the dusty little sidewalk to find out for herself how things were going for her friend.

Chapter Fourteen

Offspring

There was no one to answer her soft rapping, so Cassandra let herself in. She could detect the smell of antiseptic as soon as she entered. It made her stomach turn and she reached for a chairback to steady herself.

Everything seemed hushed. She could not even hear movement, and for one awful moment she feared that something had happened and everyone had deserted the little dwelling.

Just as she was about to panic she heard a groan and then soft, encouraging words. She recognized the voice as that of Samuel's. He was still there. He was busy with Virginia. The baby had not arrived. She should not have come.

She was about to turn and leave as quietly as she had come when the room beyond the little kitchen seemed to come to life. There was an exclamation of three excited voices and then Cassandra heard a strange new sound. Was it a baby crying?

Samuel's voice rang out clearly then. "You have a new son. A nice big fellow. Congratulations."

And then the voice of Morris. "It's a boy, Virginia. Another boy. Thank you, God. Thank you." The new father sounded close to tears.

Cassandra lowered herself onto a kitchen chair, leaned her head on her folded arms, and began to weep.

When Samuel came to the room with the new baby

wrapped in the softness of a towel, he found her there. Surprised at discovering her, he asked quickly, "Are you all right?" He wished he could go to her. But the baby needed his full and immediate attention.

Cassandra burst into fresh tears, but she managed to shake her head.

"Virginia has a fine new boy," Samuel went on, hoping to divert her attention. "Do you wish to see him?"

Cassandra sat upright, dabbed at her eyes and nodded her head. She did want to see Virginia's new baby. She rose from her chair and crossed to where Samuel had lowered his bundle and was working over the baby, who still protested his new surroundings.

But Cassandra was not prepared for what she was about to see. All babies that she had seen had been clean and pink and dressed in soft gowns of white cotton and lace. This one was nude. Nude and red and covered with blood and an ugly film of—of something. She felt her stomach heave again.

"What's wrong with him?" she managed to blurt out before she reached for the support of the chairback.

Samuel's head came up. "Nothing," he replied quickly. "He's—perfectly healthy."

"But he—he looks so—"

"Oh that," and Samuel laughed. "That's how all babies look when they enter the world. That's God's protective blanket."

Cassandra managed to make her way back to the chair. She feared that she was going to get sick.

She sat holding her head and waiting for the nausea to pass.

"This is Anthony Daniel," Samuel informed Cassandra over the cry of the infant. "He isn't too happy with his new world right now, but he'll feel much better once we get him cleaned up and back to his mama."

And Samuel continued doing whatever it was he was doing to the infant, talking to the wee boy as he worked, pleased with the healthy baby, the world in general, and his profession in particular.

"I won't be long now," he said to Cassandra. "Wait and say hello to Virginia. I'll call you as soon as she is ready."

Cassandra managed a nod, but she wondered if she would be able to walk into the medicinal-smelling bedroom and greet her friend.

Then Samuel bundled the baby, tucked him under his arm, his hand supporting the tiny head, and headed back to the bedroom.

Cassandra could hear the "ohs" and "ahs" of excited exclamations as the proud parents carefully examined their new son.

"Look! Look!" cried Virginia. "He's sucking his fist."

"It's his thumb. He's got his little thumb right in his mouth. Look at that, would you. Look here, Doc," said Morris excitedly, "Anthony Daniel is already sucking his thumb."

Cassandra heard chuckles and cooing and knew that the whole room had already forgotten the ordeal of the preceding hours.

"Cassandra is here," Samuel said at last. "I think she is anxious to see you and the baby."

Samuel could not have known the falsehood. Her very appearance in the house seemed to prove his statement. Cassandra knew that the time had come for her to draw strength from beyond herself and visit the room used for delivery, or else pass out on the kitchen floor.

She breathed a quick but sincere prayer as Samuel's footsteps approached, and rose shakily to her feet. She was ready to give hearty congratulations to Virginia.

―――――

Cassandra continued to receive letters from home, which she always answered immediately. If her mother detected a change in her attitude over the months, she did not make comment. Cassandra herself did not realize how much difference her submission to God and her friendship with Virginia was influencing her outlook on life.

―――――

When Cassandra's turn came to deliver, Samuel was making a house call in the country. Though Cassandra did not know exactly where he was, she had been given strict instructions to get word to Morris at the drugstore via one of the neighbor children, should she feel the least twinge of labor. Unknown to her, Samuel carefully reported his whereabouts to Morris several times during the day so that he could always be found quickly.

Cassandra waited until she was sure the pains were actual contractions, then walked the short distance to the neighbor's house.

"I think the time has come," she said simply when the woman answered her knock. The lady nodded and turned to call, "Jake. Jake, ya there?"

A boy answered.

"Run on down to the drugstore and let Mr. Foigt know it's time."

Cassandra heard the back door slam before she even turned from the front door.

"Thank you," she called over her shoulder, but Mrs. Hardy was right at her elbow.

"How far apart?' she asked Cassandra.

Cassandra frowned. She wasn't sure what the woman was talking about.

"How far apart are the contractions?" asked the woman again.

"Well, they are about from here to here," replied Cassandra, indicating the area on her broad abdomen.

Mrs. Hardy began to laugh.

"I meant, how many minutes apart," she corrected.

Cassandra flushed. "I—I don't know. I haven't paid any heed," she admitted.

"Well, we'll time 'em," said the woman as she purposefully took Cassandra's arm to assist her in climbing the steps to her home.

They were barely settled in Cassandra's bedroom when the next contraction came. Mrs. Hardy laid a hand on Cassandra's tightened stomach. "Nice and strong," she said, seeming pleased.

Cassandra laid back against the pillow when the contraction ended. She wasn't sure that she shared the pleasure. The pain had been quite sharp.

She relaxed again and was content to allow Mrs. Hardy help her slip out of her dress and into a comfortable nightgown. Then the woman busied herself about the room, making Cassandra feel strangely comforted and uncomfortable at the same time.

The comfort came because the woman was company and also because she seemed so relaxed, so knowledgeable about what should be done. The uneasiness came because she seemed to be preparing for a delivery—and Samuel was to be present for that. Cassandra began to fret that Samuel might not make it home after all.

But he did. He arrived breathless and flushed. She knew by his face that this was a bit different for the young professional. This was his wife. His baby.

"How are you?" he asked Cassandra, brushing her red hair back from her face, but before Cassandra had answered he turned to Mrs. Hardy. "How is she?"

"About ten minutes apart. Nice and firm, though. It's labor all right."

Then Samuel turned back to Cassandra and gave her his full and undivided attention, while Mrs. Hardy went to the kitchen to put on a pot of coffee.

———

Joseph Henry arrived at one-thirty in the morning, after what seemed to Cassandra a very long time. But Samuel appeared well pleased with the progression of events. And as soon as baby Joey was placed in her arms, Cassandra was willing to admit that the whole experience was worth it. She loved him instantly, from the tip of his perfect ten toes to the top of his reddish fuzzy head. As he nestled up against her and seemed to snuggle himself in against her breast, she would not have traded him for all the treasures of the world. She was sure her father would be pleased to hear that he had a grandson bearing his name. She did wish she could have the privilege of sharing her joy in person with her far-away parents.

————

The two young mothers now had even more to share. Though their babies kept them busy, they made time for visits back and forth. Cassandra dreaded winter anyway, but now she was afraid that the cold would keep her homebound with young Joseph.

"He'll be fine if you bundle him up," Samuel assured her. "Fresh air is healthy. He should have outings."

Following the doctor's advice, Cassandra took full advantage of the milder days and brought Joseph with her to visit Virginia and Anthony and even over to the church while she practiced the Sunday hymns. He seemed to love the music of the complaining, rasping old instrument, and Cassandra would smile as she played and her baby cooed.

————

Cassandra couldn't help but be disappointed when she discovered she was pregnant again.

"I wanted Joey to be my baby for a longer time," she fretted. "He's only a year old. He will need to grow up before he should."

Samuel looked at his growing son, trying to pull himself up by the chair rungs. "Maybe God knows that he will be ready for a brother, Red," he replied.

But it wasn't a brother. It was Vivian Ann. And if Cassandra had felt busy before, she was doubly so now.

————

Joseph seemed to go from being a baby to a young boy

before Cassandra had time to make the mental adjustment. One day he was cooing in her arms and the next, it seemed, he was insisting on playing outside where he could have freedom to run and explore.

Cassandra had to constantly watch him, chase him, bring him home from a venture, rescue him from climbs, warn him about dangers. It was a constant demand on her time and attention.

Samuel noticed her difficulties and hired a man to build a swing so the toddler would have something to do close to home. He also provided a sandbox and small pails and shovels. But the special play things drew the neighborhood youngsters. Cassandra was happy to have playmates for her son, but it meant a constant vigil on the gate leading to the yard. Children were always forgetting to close it. Cassandra feared that they might one day leave it open and Joseph would wander at will. Dozens of times daily she checked the gate. And dozens of times daily she closed it herself, then reminded the neighborhood children to please close it as they entered or left. They always nodded their agreement and promised faithfully to fulfill her request, but again and again Cassandra found the gate swinging in the summer wind.

One day when Cassandra went to shut the gate, she found an empty sandbox, a lifeless swing—and no Joseph.

Panic seized her. She rushed to the street and looked first one way and then the other. Only a team of plodding horses moved before her eyes. The old gentleman driving lifted a hand and called a cheery greeting. Cassandra tried to respond, but her frantic thoughts were on her missing son.

She was about to dash off down the street looking for him when she remembered little Vivian. She hurried back to the bedroom, picked up the sleeping baby from her cradle, and rushed back out into the street.

"Perhaps the Hardys'," she said, and ran to the house next door. But no one was home, and as Cassandra looked around the yard, she saw no trace of Joseph.

On she went from one neighbor to another, from one yard to another, but she found no Joseph, nor anyone who had seen the small boy. People soon joined her in the search. Children dashed on ahead to see if they could be the first one to find the missing child. Women walked along beside her, trying to give words of encouragement, assuring her that he couldn't have gone far. Men left their work and fanned out in another direction so more ground could be covered faster.

Someone brought word to Samuel, and he met Cassandra on the street and relieved her of the baby, who was now feeling that she should be fed.

"I just left him a few moments," sobbed Cassandra. "I had checked the gate only a few minutes before."

"We'll find him," Samuel tried to assure her and then repeated the words that had become so familiar to her, "He couldn't have gone far."

Cassandra wanted to scream.

Baby Vivian began to fuss more insistently. "It's time for her to eat," admitted Cassandra as Samuel handed her back to her mother.

"Why don't you go home and feed her? We'll all keep looking. I'll bring him on home just as soon as we find him," Samuel urged. With tears on her own face, Cassandra took the crying baby and headed for home.

The day was hot and she felt exhausted from the heat and the worry and terribly angry with herself for not having kept a better eye on her son.

Vivian cried harder and Cassandra felt like sitting down right on the sidewalk and nursing her baby girl. She couldn't stand the crying. Couldn't stand her anguish. Couldn't stand the thought that her young son might be in real danger. She wanted to draw her baby girl close and get at least a measure of comfort from her soft little body.

But Cassandra plodded on home—through the heat, through the dust, her heart heavy and her back aching.

"Oh, God!" she cried. "I admit that it was my fault. I should have watched more closely. But please—please—let him be okay. Help us to find him. Help us, please, God. Please!"

Cassandra followed their wooden sidewalk through the

offending gate, which still swung open, and headed for her back door. She would be so thankful to get in out of the heat. She would be so thankful to sit after walking for what seemed forever. She would be so thankful to be able to hold her baby close and give her the comfort of nursing. But oh, how she ached and longed for her lost son. The nearer she drew to her own door, the more the tears flowed.

She was about to open the door and step through to the kitchen when she heard a noise. It came from the corner of the yard where the sandbox was located. She turned, thinking it to be one of the neighborhood children, but there sat Joseph. He was busy with a small shovel, scooping up sand to fill a little box he had found somewhere. He was totally absorbed in his play, not even noticing his mother until she cried his name and ran toward him. When he did lift his head, he grinned a happy grin and went back to filling his box.

"Joseph!" cried Cassandra again. "You're home. You're home! Where have you been?"

The little red head lifted again and he held out his shovel toward his mother. "Yook" was his only comment.

Cassandra saw his torn shirt, his dirt-smeared face, a shoeless foot. But she concentrated only on his sparkling hazel eyes. He was home! He was whole! She hugged him to her as she thanked God, and baby Vivian protested loudly.

They never did learn where Joseph had been. The missing shoe was never found.

Chapter Fifteen

Experiences

Cassandra stood at the kitchen cupboard peeling potatoes for the evening meal. Joseph played in the yard with neighborhood children. At four, he now understood that he was not to leave his yard without his mother's permission.

When Cassandra heard him cry out she turned from the potato pan, wiping her hands on her apron as she rushed toward the back door. In the process she nearly tripped over young Vivian, who was playing with her doll baby on the floor.

"Oh my!" she exclaimed. She didn't know whether to take Vivian with her or leave her and run to Joseph. She was slow enough now in her movements with a third child soon to join the family.

"You stay put, sweetie," she said to Vivian and rushed out.

When Cassandra reached the play yard she was totally unprepared for what greeted her. Joseph sat screaming on the ground, his hands holding his head, and between his fingers oozed blood that dripped on his shirt front. Cassandra was sure he must be about to breathe his last.

"What happened?" she screamed at the neighborhood children who gathered around, speechlessly observing the flow of blood.

It seemed to bring Robert, one of the children, back to coherence. "The swing hit him," he cried, and then the others began to respond with excited yells and even wilder swinging of their arms to show what had happened.

Cassandra reached for Joseph who was still screaming at the top of his lungs.

"Someone run for the doctor!" shouted Cassandra, but everyone stared at her wildly.

"Run for the doctor," she repeated, lifting the bleeding boy into her arms and running for the house.

Vivian had followed her mother out the door and was standing on the steps. As soon as she saw her brother with his face covered in his own blood, she too began to cry. Cassandra didn't know what she would do with another frantic child. Nor did she know where or how badly her son was hurt. From the amount of blood all over his shirt and now on the front of her as well, she thought he must be seriously injured. She hoped and prayed that one of the children had obeyed her cry and gone for help.

"Come with Mama," Cassandra urged Vivian, opening the door and following the child in.

She stood holding the boy, looking out the window for someone to come to her aid. She didn't know how to care for him. Samuel was the doctor. Cassandra had never been able to stand the sight of blood. All she could do was to rock him gently in her arms, to comfort him. It didn't work and soon Cassandra was crying right along with her two offspring.

A heavy step pounded across the back porch and Samuel burst into the house. "What happened?" he asked as he reached for Joseph.

"The swing!" cried Cassandra. "He got hit with the swing. He's hurt badly, Samuel. He's bleeding—"

"Head cuts always bleed a lot," Samuel interrupted her; then seeing her pale face, he nodded toward a kitchen chair. "You'd better sit down."

Cassandra managed to get the chair under her and leaned down to scoop Vivian into her arms. "Sh-h," she whispered, trying to soothe her. "Sh-h. Papa's here now. Joey will be all right."

Samuel grabbed a clean towel from a kitchen drawer and began to wash the boy to determine the location and extent of injury. Joseph screamed even louder and Vivian joined in. Cassandra felt as if she were going to smother from the tension.

"Hush," she heard Samuel say rather sternly to young Joseph. "Let me look at your cut. Don't fuss so."

For some strange reason, Joseph seemed to listen to his father and the wild screams changed to whimpers. Vivian, too, quieted her crying, though she still clung to Cassandra.

"It's not too bad," Samuel the doctor was saying. "It's not deep—but it will need some stitches or it will scar."

Then he turned to Cassandra. "I might need your help. Do you feel up to it?"

Cassandra looked at him with large, startled eyes.

"Me?"

"I need someone to hold his hands while I stitch. One wild sweep of a hand could do more damage than the swing did," he explained calmly.

Cassandra eased Vivian away from her and stood to shaky feet. She took one tentative step and then another and soon she was beside Samuel, looking down at her son. He did look much better now that Samuel had washed away much of the blood, but the open wound on his forehead still seeped bright red liquid. Cassandra felt her knees giving way and she bowed in prayer and asked God for His strength for the task ahead.

Joseph lifted his eyes to study her face. She managed a wobbly smile. She even managed to speak. "Papa has to sew up the cut," she said evenly, firmly, "and it is very important that you hold still and not bump his hand. Do you understand? Mama is going to help you keep your hands perfectly still. We'll put them both here—on your chest—and Mama will put her hands here." She took the hands of the child firmly in her own. "Now, you watch me—not Papa."

Out of the corner of her eye Cassandra could see the needle with its trailing thread in Samuel's fingers. Again she thought her knees would surely buckle under her, and she prayed and willed the dizziness from her whirling head.

"What do you want to do after Papa is all done?" she asked

Joseph, wanting to keep his full attention.

"I want to play with Anthony again," the boy said without hesitation.

"Well, it's almost suppertime," said Cassandra, attempting a matter-of-fact tone in her voice. When she had first arrived in the little prairie town, she had vowed she would never, never change the evening meal from dinner to supper. But she had. In fact, over the months that she had lived in the West, many things had been slowly changing in the life and thinking of Cassandra.

"Anthony's mother might want him home," she went on to explain.

Joseph looked about to cry again and Cassandra quickly amended her statement. "But we'll see. There might be time to play for a while yet."

Samuel made another stitch. The boy seemed to pay little attention.

"What will you and Anthony play?" asked Cassandra, trying hard to buy some time. She prayed that Samuel was almost done.

"In the sandbox—with my little wagon," answered the boy.

Then his eyes shifted from Cassandra to his father, and he noticed for the first time the hand that held the needle, with its thread now red from his blood.

At first his eyes grew wide as though he couldn't understand the implication, but he quickly sorted it out and just as quickly began to shriek. Now Cassandra's strength was pitted against her son's. He tried to free his entrapped hands so that he might fight to protect himself, and it was all that Cassandra could do to hold him. With a few more quick stitches Samuel finished the job and Joseph was wiped off, bandaged, and freed to stand on his own.

Tears still ran down his cheeks, and he looked at both his parents for as much sympathy as they could possibly muster. It was then that Cassandra noticed Vivian. She stood on a kitchen chair, her head craned so she could see better, her eyes wide with the wonder of it all. She was not crying; she was not even pale. She looked as though she had been wonderfully captivated by the whole procedure.

When Samuel snapped shut his medical bag, she looked at him pleadingly. "Fix him some more, Papa," and waved a chubby hand in Joseph's direction.

Samuel and Cassandra exchanged glances, then began to chuckle as Samuel reached for his small daughter and hugged her.

"So you will be Papa's nurse, will you?" he said, giving her a few sound pats on her solid bottom. "I guess I should have had *you* holding brother's hands instead of your poor mama."

Joseph had stopped crying and reached up a hand to feel his bandage.

"You bleed, Joseph," Vivian informed him, and her voice held a note of excitement as though bleeding was something quite special.

Joseph grinned and Cassandra breathed a little prayer. "It's over. Thank you, God."

"You even bleed on Mama," went on the girl and pointed with her stubby finger.

Cassandra looked down to where the little finger was pointing and saw that her blouse billowing around their next child was also covered with Joseph's blood. Such red, red blood.

She felt her knees going weak again and this time she was totally unprepared and there was no stopping her. Had Samuel not been there to grab her, she would have collapsed on her kitchen floor.

That night Christina Marie was born. Though two weeks early, she was wiry and seemingly unscathed by the day's events. She had a powerful set of lungs, and Cassandra lay back on her pillow and wondered what on earth she would do if all three of them should decide to cry at once.

She managed to sleep after the birthing and opened her

eyes later to find the room quiet and the baby sleeping soundly beside her. Everything seemed so still it was eerie, and then she remembered that Samuel had said he would take the two older ones to Virginia so the exhausted new mother might get some rest. She closed her eyes and slept again.

When the door opened later and Samuel came in to stand beside the bed, Cassandra looked up from the infant daughter sleeping in the curl of her arm.

"Is she all right?" she asked frankly.

"She's just fine," he assured her again as he had many times since the baby's arrival.

"She's smaller than the others," observed Cassandra.

"Give her a couple weeks—the time she should have arrived—and she will likely pass both of their birth weights," he promised.

Cassandra smiled at her baby.

"I got the wire off to your folks," he said, rubbing his hands together because the early morning air held a chill.

Cassandra lifted her eyes to his.

"Mama will think I do nothing but have babies," she said in a soft voice.

"Do you mind?" asked Samuel.

"Mind?" Cassandra turned her head to kiss the warm little bundle that rested against her. "They're beautiful babies" was her answer. She hesitated for a moment, then went on softly, "And they have a wonderful father." She reached out to squeeze his hand. "And I have a wonderful doctor," she said with teasing in her voice.

————

That summer, Samuel decided it was time to add on to their house. With three little ones underfoot, they needed more room. The construction time was a real trial to Cassandra. Besides the prairie dust that yearned to seep in through every small crack around doors or windows, she now had the added dust from saws and hammers. There was also the noise. It seemed that just as soon as she managed to get a child to sleep, the din would start, waking the little one again.

She knew that in time she would be thankful for the additional room, but there were many days when Cassandra frankly wondered if it was really worth it.

Finally the last board was cut, the last nail hammered, the last swish of paint brushed on the new walls, and Cassandra was free to clean up the mess and move her simple furnishings into their proper places.

She heaved a sigh of relief. Perhaps it had been worth it after all. It certainly was nice to be able to move around without bumping one's shins on small beds.

———

Cassandra sat with her friend Virginia in the shade of the back porch as they sipped cool lemonade from tall glasses. Nearby their offspring played together. They were "even" again with the birth of Virginia's third son, but the two youngest, Christina and James Samuel, slept beside their mothers. They were still much too young to be interested in the sandbox.

"It's a good thing that Christina joined Vivie," Virginia mused, "or she would be terribly outnumbered."

Cassandra nodded, then added truthfully, "She doesn't seem to mind. She plays with the wagons and little animals about as much as she does with dolls."

"Yes, but she is different."

"Tougher," agreed Cassandra, and they both laughed.

They sat in silence for a time enjoying the antics of their playing children. Then Virginia drew Cassandra's attention with a quiet question. "Do you still miss Montreal?" she asked.

Cassandra had to think about her answer. She put down her empty glass and looked first at her friend and then at her children.

"Yes—I miss it," she finally answered honestly. "I would

love to go back. To show off my children. To enjoy some of the—the finer things. To get away from the wind and the dust. To teach my children about the—the other side of—of living."

As she spoke her voice became more and more nostalgic. She did miss Montreal. She missed her mother. And there were many days when, much to her surprise, she realized she also greatly missed her father. And she often wondered about her now-grown little brothers. They were men. Two of them had married and she had missed both weddings.

Abigail, on the other hand, seemed like some dream creature from a distant past. There were days when Cassandra almost wondered if Abigail had really existed. But of course she knew she did. She still wrote occasionally. She and her new husband seemed to move around a lot. Cassandra was never sure from where the letters might be postmarked next. It was hard to keep up with Abigail.

Yes, she did miss Montreal. She would love to go back. But much to her surprise she realized that even now she no longer struggled with a need to go back—only a desire.

"I—I guess I have adjusted—somewhat," she admitted to Virginia.

"You've grown," corrected Virginia. "I've watched it happen. You are not the young woman I first met."

Cassandra looked up in surprise, adding thoughtfully, "I guess one can't be a mother and still act like a child," she commented.

"Some women do," countered Virginia. "I've met them. I have at times wondered who would do the rearing. The mother—or the child."

Cassandra smiled. That was a bit of an exaggeration, she was sure, but she understood Virginia's point.

But Virginia changed the conversation back to her original topic. "I have never been East," she stated. "I've always thought it would be fun to go."

"Oh, you should. You'd love it. There are plays and concerts and so—so many things to do. And you can shop—until you drop," she added with a laugh, remembering how she and Abigail used to use the phrase.

"Do you think you and I could handle six babies?" asked Virginia.

Cassandra's eyebrows went up. "What do you mean?" she asked.

"Well, Morris said last night that I should get you to take me East. Get it out of my system. He said he was sure Samuel would let you go for a few weeks—to show off your babies and all. I could get a hotel room nearby, and we could spend our days in parks and maybe even find a nanny to stay with the children while we did some shopping or took in a concert or—"

But Cassandra had grabbed her hand. "Are you serious?" she asked.

"Yes. Perfectly. I don't think it sounds so impossible—do you?"

"Impossible? Of course it's impossible. The two of us with six babies? It's sheer foolishness—Oh, let's do it. Let's!"

And from then on they could think or talk about nothing else.

Chapter Sixteen

The Adventure

There was no rest for anyone until the plans were made, the cases packed, and Cassandra and Virginia, with their six small charges, were boarded on the Canadian Pacific Railroad train in Calgary, headed east for Montreal. Samuel and Morris waved them off, smiles firmly in place.

Joseph and Anthony seemed totally taken with the new venture and spent the first few hours at the window pointing out things of interest to each other. Vivian and Paul got in the game as well.

"Yook! Yook!" Paul would shout excitedly, but because his finger flew from one direction to another, no one could understand exactly what was to claim their attention.

The swaying of the train and the clacking of the wheels seemed to lull the two babies to sleep. Cassandra and Virginia looked at each other.

"This might not be so bad," said Cassandra with a smile. "We get to just sit back and relax."

But that wasn't to last for long. Vivian and Paul soon tired of the game and wished to run in the aisles instead. They were not pleased when their mothers insisted that they had to stay in their own small compartment.

Then Joseph and Anthony became restless and at about the same time the two babies awakened. The party was over—and they were barely on their way.

The long days and nights on the train proceeded in much

the same fashion. The children had their good times when
something took their attention off their cramped quarters,
and Cassandra and Virginia would breathe a collective sigh
of relief. But just as quickly the tables could turn and the
youngsters would become bored and restless and ready to
run.

"When are we gonna get there?" was asked over and over,
and Cassandra or Virginia would try to be patient as they
explained that it was some distance yet.

They took turns going to the dining car. The short trips
were the biggest events of the day. The children loved the
walk down the long train aisle. They loved to see some new
surroundings. And they loved to sit at the table and have
their mama entertain them by folding the napkins into
strange shapes while they waited for their food to arrive.

While Cassandra ate and fed Joseph and Vivian, Virginia
remained behind with her three and the sleeping Christina.
Cassandra never left while Christina was still awake. And
when Virginia took her two oldest to the dining car, Cassandra took her turn watching little James.

In theory the plan worked just fine, but they soon discovered that there were snags. Sometimes the babies both awakened while one mother was gone, and then the mama left
behind truly had her hands full.

But for the most part, the trip went rather well, though
both mothers could hardly wait for Montreal and a full
night's sleep.

They were met at the train station by Cassandra's parents. It was a joyful, tearful time and Virginia pulled back,
feeling a bit awkward at intruding on the reunion of family.

But her discomfort did not last long. "This is Virginia,"
Cassandra said, drawing her forward. "And this is Anthony,
Paul and James." Virginia and her family were greeted
warmly.

"If you will just direct me," she informed the Winstons,
"I am sure I will be able to find transportation to my hotel."

"Nonsense!" exclaimed Mrs. Winston. "We have room for
you all at the house and I wouldn't hear of you going elsewhere."

"But—," began Virginia.

"Now, no buts," said Mrs. Winston. "We want to get to know Cassandra's best friend."

"But it isn't fair to have outsiders cutting in on your family time," insisted Virginia.

Cassandra reached out and took her hand. "Oh, Virginia," she said with a little laugh, "you are no outsider."

"Besides," continued Mrs. Winston, "the children will need playmates while they are here. They would be bored to tears with just us old folks."

Virginia did not argue further but allowed them to tuck her and her family into the second carriage that pulled up to convey them to the Winston home.

On the drive through the busy streets of Montreal, Joseph and Vivian were almost beside themselves at the exciting things to see.

"Look at that! Look at that!" they kept shouting so that Cassandra could scarcely carry on a conversation with her parents. "Look, G'wamma," Vivian insisted, fitting right in to the new relationship.

Oh, dear, Cassandra thought with disappointment. *Mama will think that they have no manners at all.*

But Mrs. Winston almost seemed to delight in the many interruptions. She smiled at the excitement and explained things to the children. Even Henry P. joined heartily in the fun, exclaiming with satisfaction at the sturdiness of the boy, the rosy cheeks of his sister, and the strong grip of baby Christina. Cassandra smiled. Her papa always saw things through the eyes of a physician.

Mrs. Winston had been thorough in her arrangements. Not only did she have a nanny booked for the occasion but a nurse as well. Cassandra found herself with more freedom than she had enjoyed for years.

And her papa was generous with opera tickets and transportation and even his credit accounts. Cassandra felt delightfully pampered and spoiled.

There was only one thing wrong. She missed Samuel. She ached for Samuel. She thought of him in the morning with the first opening of her eyes. She thought of him every time she sat down to a meal of sumptuous fare. She thought of him when she attended the theater or the concert hall and wondered if he was being worked off his feet, if he was making it to Mrs. Clement's for the arranged lunches and suppers, knowing that he would not be eating properly if he was needing to fix his own meals at odd hours. Heavy thoughts kept her from enjoying her time as she might have if Samuel had been with her.

For all the enjoyment of familiar things and events, somehow they had changed.

The music didn't charm her as it always had in the past. The newer, more contemporary pieces did not soothe her spirits as the familiar classical pieces had. They sounded harsh and brassy. At times she wished to leave before a concert had even ended.

The plays did not please her either. At times she cringed at the language. It bordered on the vulgar, and she soon found herself wondering what had happened to theater. She often felt as if she owed Virginia an apology as they made their way back to the carriage after a performance.

They did go shopping, and at first Cassandra buried herself in the long tables and racks of fresh-smelling silks and satins. Even the cottons and linens drew her. But the jostling of the customers in the crowded aisles and the sharpness of the sales personnel soon had her nerves on edge. She would turn to Virginia and say, "Let's get some fresh air," and they would head for the doorway, sometimes without even making a purchase.

The sidewalks, however, were no better. There were always crowds of hurrying people there as well. The two women were jostled and bumped and hurried and harried until they were both glad to flee to the comfort of the carriage. Since it was a whole new experience for Virginia, she didn't notice anything different or any changes. Cassandra tried to explain it to her in the carriage on the way back to the house. "Or maybe most of the changes are in me," she concluded as they drew up to the front door.

But oh, it was good to see her folks. Cassandra was dreadfully grateful for the opportunity to introduce her children to the wonderful set of parents who had raised her. She was happy to be able to show her parents her beautiful children.

She was proud of her firstborn, Joseph, with his thatch of unruly red hair. The color was hers. The way it flopped forward was from his father. And the hazel eyes that alertly studied the world were from Samuel as well.

Then Vivian. Strong and sturdy and solid as a little boy should be—yet Vivian was every inch a girl. Her soft little arms could wrap around your neck and your heart at the same instant. She teased with big green eyes and pouted with protruding lip as the moods took her. But she was a delightful child, full of love and compassion and tenderness even at an early age.

And baby Christina. Though only an infant, she was already showing a personality all her own. She was a contented child, playing and cooing for hours at a time. But though she did not have her mama's red hair, she did have a temper. When Christina decided that it was time for something to be done, she wanted immediate action.

Cassandra loved her three children. She thanked God for them daily, and she also thanked Him for allowing her to bring them home to their grandparents. But long before the planned three weeks had expired, Cassandra was yearning with her whole heart to board the train heading west.

———

All her brothers managed to be home on her final Sunday. Cassandra was able to meet her new sisters-in-law.

Peggy, a pretty thing, was dainty and pert—and dreadfully spoiled. But she was fun and Stephen seemed happy, and that was good enough for Cassandra.

Pearl was sweet and gentle. She was soft-spoken and almost timid. Cassandra took to her immediately and felt that she wanted to mother her. She guessed that Pearl probably brought out the mothering instinct in most women. She noticed her own mother hovering nearby to care for Pearl's needs. And Pearl had a baby girl, only two weeks younger than Christina.

At nineteen, Simon was involved in sports and not showing much interest in settling down to just one female companion.

"Simon likes all the young ladies," Stephen teased. "He takes Jennie to the football game, Peg to the cinema, Jessie to the opera—and Meg to church on Sunday."

Simon flushed slightly but made no denial.

Cassandra liked her new sisters. For a moment she felt cheated that she would not be able to get to know them better. Then she reprimanded herself.

And what would you suggest? she thought inwardly. *You think they would be happy in your dusty, windy little town?*

She knew the answer to that without giving it more thought.

Or do you suppose you should pack up your children and your Samuel and come back East to the hustle, bustle of city streets where Samuel would not even get away from crowds if he wished to step out his own door for the evening?

To her surprise she had a ready answer for that as well. *Never! Both of us would smother.*

Cassandra sat in shock. It was true. She didn't belong in the city anymore. She didn't belong in the East. The West had won her and she hadn't even been aware of the victory. How had it happened—and when? She had no idea. She only knew that she longed to go home.

———

They could see Samuel and Morris standing on the platform as the train pulled into Calgary. Joseph was the first to spot the two, and his excited shrieks filled the passenger car. "It's Papa. It's Papa."

"Where? Where's Papa?" asked Vivian, shoving her way forward to get a better look.

"Right there. See!" cried Joseph, pointing a finger in their father's direction. At the same time, Samuel spotted them, and as soon as the train had rolled to a stop he and Morris boarded to help their wives and their children disembark.

In the excitement it was hard to concentrate on gathering everything up and getting back to the platform when they all wished to stop to hug and kiss and share news with one another.

But at length they all did manage to descend the train's stairs—and in the allotted time—before the train chugged on to places farther west.

Then began the real celebration as hugs were passed all around again and again.

"I miss you, Papa," said Vivian, wrapping her arms around Samuel's neck.

"I missed you, too, baby," said Samuel and kissed her chubby cheeks. Then Joseph had his turn and then it was time for baby Christina.

"Look at her!" exclaimed Samuel. "She has gained three pounds."

Cassandra laughed. "You doctors," she teased. "You measure everyone in pounds, inches or strength."

While the Smith family was busy with their rounds of embraces, the Foigts were also celebrating their being together again.

They spent the night at a Calgary hotel and prepared to begin their trip home early the next morning. Cassandra went to bed happy. For the first time in weeks she felt whole.

————

Thomas Samuel joined the family just after Christina had celebrated her second birthday. All the children joyfully welcomed the new baby. Joseph was even allowed to come home from school early so he might see his new brother. He was now in first grade and feeling quite grown-up, while Vivian, only one year younger and advanced for her age, could not understand why she had to remain at home when the school year began.

"To help Mama with the new baby," Cassandra had tried to explain.

"The new baby isn't even here yet," Vivian had lamented.

"Well, it will be soon now," Cassandra promised.

But Vivian was not to be swayed. "Chrissie can help you with the new baby," she offered. "She likes babies lots."

It was true. Christina did like babies. And she especially liked her new brother when he made his appearance. Cassandra had to be careful where she laid him. Christina thought she had a perfect right to pull him into her arms if she could reach him. "My bro-ver," she called Thomas and seemed to feel that he was her exclusive property.

When two years later another boy was born, they named him Peter Stephen, and Christina, who was now the oldest child at home, claimed that one too. By now, though only four, she was a big help to her mother and often spent hours entertaining the younger ones.

"I think that one is going to be a teacher," commented Samuel as he watched her one day.

But Cassandra just smiled. "Perhaps she will simply be a mother," she answered him.

Samuel nodded his head. "Perhaps. But I see teacher written all over her. Vivie, my nurse, and Chrissie, my teacher."

"Whom do I get?" asked Cassandra teasingly.

"Well, for the time being you can keep that fella you're holding," said Samuel of the nursing Peter. "But when he gets a bit older, I might claim that one, too."

———

The house grew again—this time up instead of out, as two upstairs rooms were added by putting wide dormers in the attic and finishing the space as bedrooms. The stairs had to go above the place where the basement steps went down. It made their kitchen-eating area smaller, so Cassandra asked for a bay window to make up the difference. She was pleased with the result. The room looked bigger and much lighter.

Chapter Seventeen

Changes

"Mama! Mama!" a small voice cried excitedly. "We need Papa. We need Papa. Danny cut his finger."

Cassandra turned from the pan of hot sudsy dishwater and wiped her hands on the towel over her shoulder.

"What happened?" she asked, fearing the worst.

"He pinched his finger in the gate, and he's bleeding, and we need Papa."

Cassandra didn't know whether to rush to the aid of the small neighbor boy, or try to calm Christina.

"Where is he?" she asked.

"I don't know. He just—just grabbed his bag an' went."

"No—I don't mean your father. I mean Danny. Where is Danny?"

"Don't ya hear 'im?"

Cassandra opened the door and she did hear him. The crying was coming from out near the swing. She hurried toward the sound.

Danny was seated on the grass, one hand held tenderly in the other, the tears streaming down his cheeks as he surveyed the damage.

When she knelt beside him, Cassandra was relieved to see that the cut was not a big one. In fact, it scarcely bled.

"Come, Danny," she said, coaxing him to his feet. "Come into the house and we'll clean it up and put on a bandage."

Danny wailed louder at the sound of her sympathetic

voice, but he allowed her to pick him up and carry him into her kitchen.

The two small boys, Thomas and Peter, clattered kitchen pot lids as they sat on a rug in the corner. They looked up from their playing, their eyes wide with wonder.

"Sh-h." Cassandra tried to console the crying boy. "We'll have it all taken care of in a minute—then you and Chrissie can have some cookies and milk. Would you like that?"

"They are raisin cookies," Christina soothed, raising her voice to out-do the crying.

And Cassandra, who could never stand the sight of blood, somehow managed to cleanse the wound, stop the bleeding, and bandage up the small finger with some clean rags.

By the time she was done, the tears had disappeared and Danny even tried out a smile as he looked proudly at his bandage.

"Now, the cookies and milk," said Cassandra as she lowered him to the floor and went to get what she had promised.

It hadn't been so hard. Cassandra rebuked her queasy stomach and cleaned up the mess from the doctoring.

Then she supplied the milk and cookies, and in the hope that it would settle her as well, she joined the children at the table.

It worked. Soon everyone seemed to have forgotten the little incident.

When Samuel arrived home that night, Christina was quick to share the story.

"Mama's a doctor, too," she informed him seriously.

Samuel raised his head to gaze at Cassandra. She looked up from spooning mashed carrots into young Peter and laughed softly at the surprise that showed on her husband's face.

"Danny cut his finger on the gate," she explained. "I bandaged it up for him."

She saw his expression change from surprise to satisfaction.

"I guess if Mama is going to be doctoring neighborhood hurts, I should be sure to leave her some proper equipment,"

Samuel said to Christina, but Cassandra knew that he really meant the words for her.

"I have no intention of being a threat to the neighborhood by practicing medicine," Cassandra replied in good humor. "Or of taking away any of your patients," she added, a twinkle in her eye.

Samuel spoke directly to her then. "All the same," he said seriously, "it wouldn't hurt for you to have a few supplies on hand for small cuts or mild burns or bruised knees."

"Samuel—I'm not a nurse," remonstrated Cassandra.

"No—but you are a mother—and I should have thought. Whenever I pick up my medical bag and leave, all the supplies go with me. We'll remedy that first thing in the morning."

And true to his word, Samuel made up a small medical kit and insisted upon explaining it thoroughly to Cassandra.

"In case there should be a small emergency, you will not need to wring your hands until I can get here."

She nodded stiffly and hoped fervently that she would never need it.

When it was Christina's turn to start off to school, it was almost heartrending for the "little mother." On the one hand, she was excited to be able to join Joseph and Vivian. On the other hand, she hated to leave Thomas and Peter. "I think Tommy and Petey will miss me," she said, her lip quivering.

"I'm sure they will," replied Cassandra, pulling the small girl into her arms.

"Can they come, too?" asked Christina.

"No—they have to wait to grow up a bit—just like you did," Cassandra answered.

Christina crossed to her two little brothers and placed a small hand on each of them. "You are the biggerest now, Tommy. You'll need to take care of Petey all by yourself. I'll hurry home from school just as fast as I can and I'll bring you everything I learned so you can learn it too."

Tommy looked at her with mournful eyes. "I wanna go with Chrissie," he said to Cassandra, his lower lip beginning to tremble.

Peter, at two, continued to chew the toe of the shoe he had pulled off one foot and blinked solemnly. He had no idea what the fuss was about.

"Mama, we're gonna be late," cut in Joseph, who had been told that he must wait for his youngest sister.

Cassandra's eyes glanced at the clock on the wall.

"Christina, you must go now," she told the young girl. "Thomas and Peter will be fine with Mama."

Christina was still reluctant but she allowed Vivian to take her hand, picked up her newly acquired lunch pail and started toward the door.

Thomas began to howl and as soon as Peter heard the noise he joined in. With her two brothers crying at her heels, Christina changed her mind.

She jerked her hand out of Vivian's, set down her lunch pail, and began to take off her coat.

"Christina!" said Cassandra, who was trying to comfort the boys. "You must hurry."

"It's okay," said Christina in a matter-of-fact fashion, "I'll stay home with them. I can go to school when they're all growed up."

"But you can't," corrected Cassandra. "You must go to school now."

Christina looked at her in unbelief.

"But they'll cry," she wailed and led the way. Thomas and Peter both joined in.

"Oh, great!" exclaimed Joseph with grown-up disdain. "Now, we'll all be late."

It ended up that they all walked to school together. Cassandra carried Peter and led young Thomas by the hand. Christina skipped along beside them, her lunch pail swinging at her side. Vivian chattered as they went, informing Christina all about the operations of school, and Joseph, who was terribly impatient with the whole proceeding, ran on ahead after receiving a nod of permission from his mother.

Cassandra was breathless by the time they reached the school yard. The morning bell was ringing and Vivian grabbed Christina's hand, a worried look causing her smooth brow to pucker. "Run," she prompted, "Miss Everly gets cross when we dawdle."

"Tommy can't run fast," responded Christina, clasping her young brother's hand.

"You must leave Thomas," said Cassandra firmly. "Go along to school with Vivian."

Christina stopped in her tracks and looked at her mother. "Aren't you and Tommy and Petey coming too?"

"No," said Cassandra, shaking her head. "We are going home just as soon as we have you delivered."

"But I don't want to be 'livered. I want us to share," said Christina, and the tears began to flow again as she clung to her mother.

Cassandra felt that there was nothing left to do but to march her small brood right into the schoolroom. She flushed as she faced the stern Miss Everly.

"I am terribly sorry to interrupt," she apologized. "If I could just take a minute to get Christina settled, I'll—" She stopped, not sure how to finish her plea.

But Miss Everly did not scowl as Cassandra might have expected. The stories that circulated in the community about the local school mum were only about how strict and unbending she was. She didn't exactly smile, but her eyes softened and she nodded understandingly.

"It is often difficult for them to leave their mothers the first day," she said softly.

"Oh, it isn't her mother," Cassandra was quick to explain. "It's her little brothers."

Miss Everly did smile at that.

"And these are your brothers?" she asked Christina.

Christina nodded and wiped a hand across her cheek to remove some tears.

"They look very special. Have you been helping your mother tend them?"

Christina nodded again.

"I'm sure you did a very good job. They will miss you—but now it is time for another job. You need to learn to read so that you might read them stories. Do they enjoy listening to stories?"

Christina nodded for the third time.

"I suppose there is no one they would rather have read to them than their big sister Christina. Let's you and me see how quickly we can have you doing that. Shall we?"

This time Christina did not nod. She turned to Thomas and Peter and said almost firmly, "If I'm gonna read to you I gotta learn the words. You better go on home now. Mama will take care of you 'til I get back."

With a sigh of relief and an appreciative nod toward Miss Everly, Cassandra moved toward the door, her two youngest charges in tow, and Miss Everly took Christina's hand to lead her to her desk.

"If I ever hear anyone say one more word about how strict she is, I will give them a piece of my mind," Cassandra said under her breath as she turned for one last glimpse of Christina at her desk.

———

It seemed no time at all until all five children were off to school. Cassandra's eyes misted as she watched young Peter join the others for the short walk down the town's new board sidewalks to the school.

"Lord, I'm going to need you in a new way," she admitted. "I have no idea what I'll ever do with my time." But she was to be surprised. There never seemed to be any spare time on her hands.

"I don't know what is wrong with me," she confided to Virginia. "I used to care for five little tots and still manage to get my work done—somehow. Now they are all gone for several hours of the day and it still takes all of my time to accomplish the same tasks."

Virginia laughed. "You too? I thought I was the only person in town who went through that."

"It's true that I have taken on a bit more at the church again—but not that much so it should make a difference," continued Cassandra. "I just never seem to be able to keep up."

"It's all the work they leave behind them," Virginia chuckled again. "Washing, ironing, mending—"

"And they all eat—like—" Cassandra couldn't think of a proper word, but Virginia was nodding in understanding. "I don't even have a decent amount of leftovers for another meal." They both laughed.

"I guess it's a case of the job expanding to fill the time," sighed Virginia. "My mother used to say that." Virginia didn't seem at all bothered about the situation. But then, Virginia, the serene one, never did seem bothered about anything.

Cassandra nodded, trying to copy Virginia's calm, but she wasn't pleased with herself. It seemed that she should have learned to be much more efficient.

———

"Mama, Ruthie's got a sliver."

By now it had become a common event for Cassandra to bandage cuts, tend bruises, and pick slivers. The neighborhood children often ran clear across town to get her to care for some little problem. It became easier and easier for her to do, though the sight of blood still made her feel queasy.

And then one day she had a new patient.

"Mrs. Smith," said young Randall Brown when she opened the door to his knock, "Puffy's got a sore ear."

His pet jack rabbit squirmed in his arms at the unfamiliar surroundings.

"Oh my," said Cassandra, not knowing what to do. "Oh my."

She was about to tell the boy that she was unable to do anything for Puffy when she saw the pleading look in Randall's eyes. Instead of dismissing him with a casual wave of her hand and a flimsy excuse, she opened the door wider. "Bring him in," she invited. "We'll see if there is anything we can do."

Father, she prayed silently, *I don't know a thing about animals. Help me for Randall's sake.*

It appeared to be an infected scratch. Cassandra cleaned it up as well as the squirmy rabbit would allow and rubbed on a bit of Samuel's antiseptic salve.

"That's really all I can do," she told the boy. "Here, I'll give you just a bit of this and you put a little on Puffy's ear each morning until it is all used up and we'll see what happens."

Cassandra was pleased when a beaming Randall met her in the grocery store a few days later and told her that Puffy was just fine.

Samuel teased, "I hear your practice has expanded."

Cassandra tossed her head and shot back, "Word has it that the local doctor will only treat patients who carry money in a back pocket," she countered. "Since Puffy doesn't have a back pocket—someone had to look after him."

Samuel just grinned.

"You've got quite a mama," he said to Peter, who had run to greet his father, and he reached out a hand to rough up the young boy's heavy thatch of reddish hair.

"Mrs. Smith. Mrs. Smith."

Cassandra opened her eyes slowly. She was sure someone was calling her. But it was the middle of the night. Who would be wanting her now.

"Yes," she answered sleepily, thinking it might be one of the children. "Mama's coming," and she slid out of bed and reached out a foot for a slipper.

"Mrs. Smith."

Cassandra jerked suddenly awake. The children did not call her Mrs. Smith. Someone else was asking for her attention.

"I'm coming," she called softly, hoping not to waken Samuel.

Then she remembered. Samuel had been called out some time around midnight. She couldn't remember the details. Just that they had been roused, Samuel had gotten up and dressed, she had rolled over sleepily to ask him what was wrong and he had leaned over, kissed her and told her to go back to sleep. He was needed at the Harrigans'. And she had gone back to sleep. She was used to Samuel being called away in the middle of the night.

"Mrs. Smith." There it came again. It was a man's voice and it was coming from the back door. *Someone else needs Samuel and he is already gone,* thought Cassandra in a bit of a panic. She hoped the need wasn't urgent. She had no idea how long Samuel might be.

She lit the lamp that sat on the kitchen table and hurried to the door. Mr. Stockwood from the town hardware store stood on the back porch, his hat in his hand.

"Mrs. Smith—Dr. Smith asked me if I would get word to you. He's—he's had a bit of an accident."

Cassandra reached out a hand to the doorframe for support.

"Nothing serious," he was quick to add when he saw Cassandra's face go pale.

"What happened?" she asked with a shaky voice, the lamp trembling in her hand.

The man reached out and took the lamp from her and eased her back into her own kitchen. "Sit down," he instructed. "Sit down."

She sat down. Mostly because she could no longer stand. Her knees felt wobbly and she feared she might faint.

When Mr. Stockwood seemed sure that she was settled he continued.

"He was coming home from the Harrigans'—Mis' Harrigan had a baby girl last night—an' it was pretty dark. Horse musta stumbled or shied or somethin'. Anyway, he took a tumble and Doc landed on his arm. He thinks he broke it but he says it ain't a bad break. He's down to his office tryin' to sort things out. Wanted you to know 'fore word started spreadin' around."

Cassandra felt her strength returning. She had to get to Samuel.

"Will you stay with the children?" she asked hurriedly and the man nodded dumbly, then queried, "What ya plannin'?"

"I've got to go help Samuel," she explained quickly and hurried toward the bedroom to get dressed.

"Not sure he'll be wantin' ya to do thet," the man called after her. "It's awful dark out there."

"I'll carry a lantern," Cassandra called back just as she entered the bedroom door.

She dressed as quickly as she could and soon rushed back through the kitchen.

"Stir up the fire and make yourself some coffee," she invited. "The pot is there on the shelf and the coffee is in that tin."

Then she hastened to light the lantern and left the man still shaking his head.

And all the way along the boardwalk she kept repeating the same little prayer: "Let him be all right, God. Please, let him be all right."

Chapter Eighteen

The Mishap

She was out of breath by the time she pushed open the door and entered Samuel's small office. She saw a lamp in the back room and headed directly toward it.

Samuel sat in a chair, his face scratched and pale, the sleeve ripped from his shirt and discarded, his injured arm extended on the desk before him as he tried clumsily to put on some kind of splint.

He didn't even hear her until she cried out in a muffled voice, "Oh-h, Samuel."

He looked up then, his face at first showing concern, and then he gave her an embarrassed grin.

"My horse doesn't have very good night vision," he tried to joke.

"Oh-h, Samuel." Cassandra rushed to him and set her lantern beside the lamp on his desk. "What have you done to yourself?"

"Gone and broken my arm, I'm afraid," he answered evenly, turning his attention back to the limb before him.

"Are you all right?"

He nodded his head. No tease in him now. He looked at her honestly and then replied, "As all right as one can be under such circumstances."

"Are you hurt elsewhere?"

He seemed to think about that for a minute and then replied, "I really don't think so. Just a few minor scratches and some sore bones. I'll be fine in a day or two."

Cassandra knelt beside him. She wished to take him in her arms. Wished to tend his broken body as she did the children who came to her, but there was nothing she could do. She felt helpless—inadequate.

"Does it hurt terribly?" she asked, reaching out to touch the blood that had dried on his cheek.

"I've taken something for the pain—but yes, it doesn't feel especially good."

"I wish there was something I could do," she said with deep feeling.

She had expected Samuel to say that there was nothing. That she should go home to her bed. Home to the children. But instead he raised his eyes and looked directly into her green ones. "There is, Red," he said softly.

The surprise must have shown on her face. After a moment he went on. "You can help me set this arm."

Her mouth dropped—her jaw slack. Her green eyes opened wide with fright and disbelief. She stood slowly to her feet.

"We can do it," he went on calmly. "It has to be done."

Cassandra lowered her head and closed her eyes as she reached a hand to his desk to steady herself. The whole room was spinning around.

"Shouldn't—shouldn't I send Mr. Stockwood?" she stammered.

"He doesn't know one thing more than you do," said Samuel evenly. "In fact, my guess is he knows a lot less. And—and I think that we might work better as a team. All you have to do is follow my instructions—and pay absolutely no attention to me when I groan."

Cassandra looked at him. She expected him to be teasing again and was about to scold him for making light of a bad situation. But when she saw the look on his face, she realized that he was totally serious.

"Groan?" she whispered.

He nodded. "I've set many broken bones, Cassandra. I've some idea of how this is going to feel."

Cassandra went pale again. She shakily clung to reality as the world continued to spin before her.

"Do you think we can handle it?" he asked her.

Oh, Father, I'm going to need your help as never before, prayed Cassandra quickly before she opened her eyes, licked her dry lips, and nodded solemnly.

"Then let's get to it. Bring me that medical bag. We'll set out everything we might need and I'll explain it to you."

Cassandra crossed the room on leaden feet and brought the bag to him.

"Now," he continued, "arrange the items I call for here in front of us."

With trembling hands Cassandra began to lift items from the bag as he mentioned each name. She was familiar enough with his black bag to know the proper terms. When they were neatly arranged, he rose rather unsteadily from his chair.

"I'm going to lie on the floor," he explained. "That way, if I pass out, you won't need to worry about supporting me."

It was sounding worse and worse to Cassandra.

Samuel lowered himself to the wooden floor of his office, supporting his broken arm as he did so. Cassandra heard a soft groan escape his lips in spite of his attempt to muffle it.

"Put a little ether on that cloth," he told her, "and place it in my hand. I'll try not to use it, but if I can't stand the pain I will take just a whiff."

"But—but I don't know how much to give you," protested Cassandra.

"I do," he replied.

Cassandra did as bidden. The smell of the ether made her stomach heave and her head spin.

When she had placed the cloth in Samuel's hands, arranged things in easy reaching distance, she lifted her skirt slightly, then knelt on the floor beside her husband.

"Are you ready?" he asked.

She took a big breath, breathed another quick prayer and nodded.

With Samuel giving the instructions and Cassandra

trying her hardest to follow them, the procedure began.

————

It seemed to Cassandra that it would never end, but eventually she was able to lean back, face in her hands and let sobs shake her whole frame. She feared that Samuel had passed out again, but as her tears began to flow she felt his hand lift and move as he tried to pat her reassuringly.

"You did a good job," he whispered hoarsely.

His words had a comforting effect. She managed to check her sobs and began to wipe up her face. She wasn't sure if she was wiping tears or cold sweat. As she tried to compose and tidy herself, she realized that her maze of red hair was hanging in disarray about her shoulders. She had not paused to try to pin it before she left the house. She swept it back now, trying to gather it into some kind of orderliness. She had no pins. They were lying at home on her dresser.

She noticed a discarded strip of bandage on the floor and reached for it. It made a clumsy ribbon but she managed to get her hair back out of her face.

She looked at Samuel. His deathly pale face was bathed in perspiration also. She reached for a soft cloth and began to wipe his brow gently. He opened his eyes then and looked at her. She had never seen his hazel eyes quite that color before. They looked black by the light of the lamp and she wondered if it was his pain that had darkened them.

"How are you?" she managed to ask.

"Well, I don't think I will try to walk home quite yet," he answered, but she could hear the teasing in his voice again.

She didn't know whether to scold or to smile. She brushed back the shock of hair that had fallen over his forehead and let her fingers run along the strong line of his chin.

"I'm not sure I'm ready to walk yet either," she admitted.

"You should," replied Samuel, his words slurred from the drowsiness of ether, the pain he still felt, or perhaps just his total fatigue. "The children might soon be waking."

Cassandra let her eyes wander to the window. He was

right. The sky was lightening with the coming of morning. She reached down a hand to free her skirts and stood shakily to her feet.

At first she felt unsteady, cramped and achy. It had been a long time since her legs had received proper circulation. She tried to work a few kinks from them in tentative stretches and small steps.

She brushed at her skirts but the wrinkles refused to be whisked away.

"What do you want me to do?" she asked Samuel.

"I think I can make it to the cot if you'll just help me to my feet. After I get a bit of sleep I should be fine."

She helped him up and to the cot, laid him down and removed his shoes, then brought a blanket from the cupboard shelf.

Instead of leaving him, she pulled a chair up beside the bed. He opened his eyes and said sleepily, "You need to get home and relieve poor Mr. Stockwood."

"But I can't leave—," she began.

"Sure you can. I'll be fine now. All I need is a little sleep."

"I'll send Joseph," she conceded. She crossed the room, leaned over the desk and blew out the lamp. They would need it no longer. Morning had come.

Then picking up the lantern, she blew it out as well. She looked around the room for her hat and shawl and then remembered that, in her haste, she had not worn them.

She returned to the cot to tell Samuel she would be back to see him as soon as she had fed and settled the children but found him breathing deeply and evenly. He had already fallen asleep. She leaned to kiss his forehead, took one more look at him, and left as quietly as she could.

————

"I sure could use your help," said Samuel a few mornings later as he held his breakfast coffee cup awkwardly in his left hand.

They were lingering a bit. There was really no reason to

rush. The children had left for school and Samuel was limited in what he could do.

Cassandra looked from the man to the coffee cup and back again. "You wish me to feed you now?" she asked with a hint of banter.

"No. No, I still seem to be able to take care of my stomach. But I'm not much good at the office—and the people don't seem to understand. They still keep getting sick."

"Perhaps this was God's way of slowing you down," answered Cassandra. "You've been working far too hard for far too long."

"Well, if it was His idea to slow me down, He's accomplished it quite nicely," Samuel replied without rancor.

He drummed the fingers of his good hand on the table and Cassandra recognized it as a sign of impatience.

"So how do you need my help?" she asked to change back to a positive note.

"Well, I was thinking—if I had your hands I could still help a number of the patients."

"My hands?"

"Yes. If you could come into the office I could examine and diagnose and you could—well, sort of do the work."

"Oh, Samuel," she said a bit indignantly. "You know how I hate the sight of blood."

"Not every patient comes in all bloody," he reminded her.

She put down her cup and looked at him. He was serious!

"Not for the whole day," he went on. He obviously had been giving this some thought. "Maybe a few hours in the morning—or the afternoon—while the children are in school. It certainly would be a help to the patients. Mrs. Merriwood was in yesterday, and I couldn't even re-bandage her burn. And Mrs. Granger—"

"All right," she said impatiently. "I understand the need—but I'm still not sure that I could—could—"

"Of course you could," he answered without hesitation. "You've had a crash course. Anyone who could do what you did last week could handle anything I'll have to care for."

She looked at him. Doubts still filled her mind, but she

did feel bad that there was no one to care for the ill since Samuel had broken his arm.

She stirred restlessly in her chair. "You wouldn't leave me?" she asked him.

"Not for one minute," he assured her.

"I—I could try—for a day or two and see how it goes."

That was as much of a promise as she could make him at the moment.

"That's good enough for me." He smiled at her and stood to his feet.

"Could you be in about ten?" he asked.

She couldn't help but laugh at her practical and efficient husband. She nodded and began to gather the breakfast dishes. If she was going to spend her morning nursing, she had to hurry with her household chores.

He normally left the house with his hat in one hand, his black bag in the other. Now he lifted his hat from the peg and surprised her by handing it to her.

"I've heard of women who wore the pants in the family," she teased, looking down at the hat she held in her hand, "but this is ridiculous."

He grinned, picked up his medical bag and said simply, "My mother taught me that a gentleman does not put his hat on in the house."

"So?"

"So—walk me to the door—and put the hat on me."

Cassandra began to laugh but she did as bidden. As soon as he had stepped through the door onto the back porch, he turned, kissed her and tilted his head toward her. She placed his hat on his head, pulled it down over his eyes and laughed as she returned to the dishes.

Chapter Nineteen

Assistant

At first Cassandra felt nervous and awkward as she tried to follow Samuel's careful instructions, but it wasn't long until compassion for the patient took over. Instead of praying for herself and her own ordeal of dealing with cuts and bruises and aches and pains, her prayers soon turned to petitions for those she tried to help.

"God, be with little Margaret. That is such a nasty burn and for such a little one." "Father, help old Mr. Marshall. He's almost blind and I'm not sure we can clear up the infection in his eyes. You touch him, Father." "Lord, give Mrs. Collins strength to deal with her pain each day. Her hands are so twisted I don't know how she can hold a spoon. Yet she must care for the needs of her elderly husband."

And on and on it went. Patient after patient and prayer after prayer.

Some days she came home so exhausted, emotionally as well as physically, that she began to wonder how her husband had endured all the years of intense giving.

Samuel noticed her weariness. "Let me read the children their bedtime story," he'd say, or "Vivian, Mama needs a bit more help tonight. She's had a long day."

The children did not seem to mind the tasks Samuel added to their responsibilities. It rather surprised Cassandra and made her realize that their youngsters were growing up.

Joseph had the job of bringing in wood and water for the

163

kitchen and keeping the sidewalks shoveled. The girls shared in the meal preparation, setting the table, and doing the dishes. Thomas and Peter cared for the pets, cleaned the shoes for school the next morning, and put away all toys that had been played with that day. Each child was responsible for making beds. Cassandra was never sure of their system. They worked it out among themselves, trading the job back and forth, but Cassandra never found an unmade bed after they had left for school in the morning.

The winter days passed, and Samuel assured Cassandra almost daily that his arm was healing nicely. But she didn't like the way his fingers swelled on occasion, or the fact that he moved restlessly at times when he didn't think she was looking.

At last the day came when he said the cast should come off, and the task was assigned to her. She was sure that her hand would slip and she would cut him, but somehow the plaster fell away as it was supposed to do and there was his arm again, thin and pale and ugly looking. Cassandra was not prepared for the sight and in spite of her toughening from nursing chores, she nearly fainted.

But Samuel did not seem the least concerned. He tried to move his arm, working the fingers of the hand to test the mobility.

"I think you did a good job, Red," he grinned at her.

"Samuel—it looks—looks sick," she countered, still feeling the horror of the sight before her.

"That's normal," he replied without a flinch. "It takes a while."

Cassandra turned away and cried out to God in silent prayer, "Please, God, let it be all right. We need him whole again. We have endured about as long as we can on our own strength. The family needs him now. And his patients need their doctor. I can't do what needs to be done, Lord."

When Cassandra turned back around to face Samuel, he was still flexing his fingers, working them this way then that—tightening, relaxing, lifting, bending.

"Needs a little exercise and it will be as good as new," he

assured her, and Cassandra prayed that he might be right.

Cassandra did not get back to her kitchen duties as quickly as she had hoped. Samuel still needed her in the office. His fingers were getting more usable, his arm a bit stronger, his hand able to accomplish one more little task with each passing day, but the progress still seemed to be painfully slow.

So Cassandra hurried through her morning chores and went to the office for a few hours each morning and again in the afternoon.

"I don't know how you do it," said Virginia one day as she placed two of her freshly baked pies on Cassandra's kitchen table. "Here I am at home all day and I can hardly keep up."

Cassandra sighed and poured steaming tea from the china teapot.

"I'm not doing much of a job of it either," she admitted dourly. "I feel that the children are being cheated of a mother—and the people of the town are being cheated of a doctor."

She sat down heavily in her chair. She was tired.

"Nonsense," said Virginia. "The children have never said one word to me about feeling cheated. In fact, I think they really are quite proud of you. I heard Chrissie boasting to her friends the other day about your care of the little girl with the dog bite."

Cassandra paled at the mention of the case. It had been horrible, and it had been all that she could do to follow Samuel's orders in the stitching. But Samuel's fingers still did not work properly, and the child would have been terribly scarred had the stitching not been done. Even now, Cassandra prayed that God would take her bungled work and perform His own miracle.

Samuel had praised her work. "I couldn't have done better." Then he had teased. "Your mama's lessons in needle-work have paid off."

Cassandra was too drained of energy to have a quip ready in response.

"I just hope her arm won't be too scarred," she managed to say to Virginia now.

"Her mother is most pleased with how it is healing," said Virginia and stirred sugar in her tea.

"You know, Virginia, if it wasn't so totally exhausting, I might even—well, not enjoy—but at least get satisfaction from working with Samuel. When you see the needs of the people—well, I have learned to understand why he feels the way he does about practicing medicine."

Virginia nodded. "I can well understand," she said simply. "I sometimes wish I had something that important to give."

———

The words stayed with Cassandra as she unpinned her hair and let it fall about her shoulders. There were a few gray hairs among the red. Her mother had told her that red-headed people sometimes grayed prematurely. Cassandra studied the strands and mused, "Am I graying early, or am I really that old?"

She did not wish to answer her own question. But she had noticed no sign of gray among Samuel's heavy locks.

She turned her thoughts back to Virginia's words. *Something important to give.* She repeated them again and again to herself, trying to discover and sort out the full meaning. *I wonder if any human being really has something more important to give than another—or is it just a little less showy,* she pondered.

"I know Samuel is important to the people of town," she murmured, "and Morris with his drugstore, and Pastor and Mrs. Ray—but I wonder if old Mr. Marshall with his watery eyes and shaky hands isn't giving just as much in another way. The children love his stories and he always has time for them."

Samuel came in just then and looked inquiringly at her. "I'm just wondering," she explained, "what it means for people to have something important to give." He still looked puzzled, and she went on. "Like Mr. Stockwood, for instance. Can't imagine how many folks he's helped by providing nails and screens and doorknobs and butcher knives. And Miss Everly, with her stern ways but her real love for the children she teaches—and even Mrs. Clement, with her sharp tongue and sharper eyes. I know there's a good many times that she gave me cause to think. Is any one of these people more important than the other?" She paused and Samuel watched her face carefully.

"No, I don't think so," Cassandra answered her own question. "We just have different roles to play—but if we are doing our job properly, then God uses our bit to help the whole. We all have something important to give. Whether it be little in our own eyes or in the eyes of others, or whether it be great. I know that Virginia has certainly given generously to me over the years. I don't know if I could have struggled through those first years without her, and her wise and continual spiritual encouragement—I need it even now. And she watches the children when I have to help in the office. I know that if I'm not around when they come home from school, Virginia will be watching out for them. That's been a real comfort on busy days."

Samuel came over and put his arms around her.

When they prayed together before retiring that night, Cassandra said, "Thank you, Father, for Virginia. And for Pastor and Mrs. Ray, and old Mr. Marshall and even Mrs. Clement—and every member of this little town—this community. We need one another. Might we never forget to give our 'important something' for the good of us all."

Samuel's "amen" echoed hers.

————

After another exhausting day, Cassandra and Samuel arrived home from the office one evening to find five forlorn children sitting on the back step.

"You can't go in the kitchen," said Peter, happy he could be first to tell the news. "It's full of smoke."

"Did you have a fire?" asked Samuel, concern edging his voice. Cassandra rushed on ahead to peer through the window at the damage.

It was difficult to see in the room, for the smoke still hung heavy in the air.

"What happened?" asked Cassandra, fearing the worst.

"Vivie," said Thomas simply.

"Vivie, what happened?" demanded Cassandra. "Are you hurt?"

Vivian seemed unsure if she should cry, beg mercy, or thrust out her chin in defiance. She chose to do all three.

"I was baking," she said with a sob, her chin lifting with a stubborn set. "I didn't mean to burn it."

"Is that all?" said Cassandra with a sigh of relief.

"She used all your eggs," accused Thomas.

"She was making an angel cake," said Peter proudly.

"Angel food cake," corrected Vivian in spite of her tears and with strong emphasis on the missing word. Joseph sat a little apart, looking disgusted with the whole affair. Christina, with motherly concern, had been trying to comfort them all.

"Where did you learn about an angel food cake?" asked Cassandra curiously as she leaned over to brush away Vivian's tears with her hankie.

"I heard Mrs. Stockwood telling Mrs. Clement. She said they are delicious and that you use lots of eggs and beat and beat—"

"She used all the eggs," put in Thomas again.

"Angel food cakes are difficult to bake," said Cassandra, straightening up and tucking away her hankie. "You should have waited for Mama—"

"But I couldn't," wailed Vivian, the tears flowing again. "It was a surprise cake."

"A surprise cake?" asked Samuel.

"For Mama's birthday," said Vivian, as though that should explain everything.

"It's not my birthday," said Cassandra.

Vivian's defiance returned. "I heard Papa say to Mrs. Foigt, 'See if you can discover what Cassandra would like for her birthday,' " she said with her nose rising into the air. "I heard it myself."

Samuel began to laugh and Cassandra looked at him in surprise and then began to laugh along with him.

"Mama's birthday isn't for three weeks yet," he informed the children.

"Then why did you say it?"

"Because I wanted to know ahead so that if I needed to order from Calgary, I would have plenty of time," answered Samuel and reached out a hand to draw Vivian up against his side.

"She used all the eggs," Thomas tried again.

But Cassandra didn't seem to hear him.

"Thank you for thinking about me, honey—even if it didn't work out well," and she gave her daughter a hug.

"I told her she should have made sugar cookies," said Christina with a slightly know-it-all tone. "She knows how to do those."

"Or ginger snaps," put in Peter. "She never burned her ginger snaps yet."

"What will we do for supper?" groused the practical Joseph, who had arrived home, tired and hungry, from his after-school job at Mr. Stockwood's store.

"Well—it might be a good night to eat at the hotel," suggested Samuel and got a roar of approval. "In the meantime I'll open the windows and see if we can clear some of the smoke out of the kitchen."

And Samuel went to open up the house.

"It's breezy," he said when he joined the family. "And I

opened the windows straight through. Perhaps it will clear things out a bit."

Yes, thought Cassandra. *If there is one thing that we can count on here, it's the breeze.*

"Well, let's go," said Samuel, "or we'll miss our supper."

To which Thomas replied dourly, "We might have to stay there for breakfast, too. She used all the eggs."

Samuel's hand was becoming more usable every day. Cassandra dared to hope that he would soon be able to handle the office on his own and she could return to her housework.

But for the time being, he still needed her hands occasionally, and she felt that it was wise for her to be available as much as possible.

The community folks were quite accustomed to seeing her in the doctor's office and no one questioned her right to be there.

In fact, neighbor women were beginning to stop her on the street or in the grocers to ask what they should do for Johnnie's cough or Mary's fever. Cassandra hardly knew how to respond. She didn't wish to dismiss the illness casually or seem unconcerned. At times she answered with a response she had heard Samuel give a patient for a similar malady, always adding that if they felt further concern to bring the patient to the office where Samuel might see him.

They always nodded their heads in complete agreement, seeming to feel that the matter had been properly attended to.

This concerned Cassandra and she discussed it with Samuel, who seemed to feel that the "switch" of doctors held no threat to the community. "If they really need me, they'll call," he said with confidence, but Cassandra still felt uneasy and on several occasions made sure that Samuel himself popped by the house in question and took a look at the patient.

But it was little Ross Hansen who renamed Cassandra.

It happened one day when the office waiting room seemed to hold more patients than usual. Cassandra had just helped Samuel extract a nasty sliver from the small boy's hand. Samuel then proceeded with the bandaging, a task he was now able to do easily.

As the boy and his mother turned to leave the office, she said to her son, "Say thank you to Doc."

The lad turned his big brown eyes, now dry of all tears, toward Samuel and said a rather shaky, "Thank you, Doc."

Before Samuel could answer, the child turned to Cassandra. "Thank you, Mrs. Doc," he said solemnly.

Laughter rippled around the room and Cassandra smiled at the wee boy.

"You are welcome, Ross. I hope your finger gets better quickly."

When the door closed on the pair, the people in the room enjoyed a chuckle again—and the name stuck.

Chapter Twenty

Mothering

It felt good to be back in her own kitchen without the requirement of going to Samuel's office daily. But Cassandra found that she never felt quite the same about Samuel's occupation after serving with him for that period of time.

When he came home at night, tired from a heavy work load, Cassandra was anxious to hear about every patient he had treated, their problem and his cure. Sometimes she feared she might tax him with all her questions, but he never seemed to mind sharing the day's happenings—though, now and then, his answer was simply, "Confidential," and Cassandra just went on to another topic.

As one season followed another and one year pushed the past one off the wall calendar, Cassandra saw her family grow up before her eyes.

It didn't seem possible to her that Joseph, their oldest, was about to finish high school. He had switched jobs now and was no longer working for Mr. Stockwood after school, but for Mr. Hick, a local builder. Joseph seemed to love to swing the hammer and only came to his father with one mashed thumb.

Mr. Hick had not been very sympathetic about the thumb. "Best way to learn," he said dryly. "Ya git one good whack and ya never leave it in the wrong place agin."

Cassandra wasn't sure it was a necessary lesson, and her mother-heart gave a sharp lurch as she looked at Joseph's bruised and bleeding thumb.

But the mishap did not deter him. Before it had barely begun to heal he was back at the construction site.

"That's where the money is," he told his parents with youthful confidence.

But Cassandra had other dreams for young Joseph.

"Do you think we should send Joseph back East for his education?" she asked Samuel as they prepared for bed one evening.

Samuel thought about it and then replied, "What do you have in mind?"

"Well—perhaps a doctor like his father and grand-father—or a—an attorney. We need more attorneys—or even a teacher or—"

"Have you talked to him about his future?" asked Samuel.

"No," admitted Cassandra. "Have you?"

"Not really—though I hear his enthusiastic reports now and then."

"You mean—construction?"

Samuel nodded his head and removed his tie.

Cassandra turned her face to study her husband. A tiny bit of gray was beginning to show at his temples. She thought it becoming. But he still looked almost boyish with his forward lock of hair.

"Really, Samuel," she said. "Do you think construction is wise? I mean—do you really think that one's livelihood could be counted on in that field?"

"I don't know," replied Samuel thoughtfully. "There's an awful lot of building going on. The boy's right. Some people are getting rich."

It sounded very "iffy" to Cassandra, even though she knew their own small town had grown a good deal since she had entered it as a young bride close to twenty years earlier. *Not that builders aren't good people and all,* she reasoned with herself, *but it's such a rough and tumble life. And Joseph has a good mind. . . .*

"What do you think we should do?" asked Cassandra aloud.

"I think we should talk to the boy and see what he thinks he wants to do with his life," responded Samuel.

"You know what he'll say," said Cassandra, her feelings still negative.

"What?" asked Samuel innocently and tossed his white shirt in the laundry basket.

"He'll say construction," responded Cassandra.

"If he's got his mind made up for construction, then he won't make a very good doctor," replied Samuel, and that seemed to settle the matter.

———

As soon as he had graduated from the local school, Joseph started into construction full time with Mr. Hick. The gentleman had been right. Joseph never came home with a banged-up thumb again.

He loved the work even though he was often so tired he could scarcely drag himself to the supper table. Vivian, who considered herself quite a young lady, often complained at the way he smelled, but Joseph would only smile and answer smartly, "It's the smell of money. Don't you recognize it?"

"It's the smell of disgusting sweat," she would reply, tossing her head much as her mother had at one time been wont to do.

"I worry about Joseph," Cassandra said to Samuel one day. "He seems terribly obsessed with amassing wealth."

But when a visiting missionary had a service in the local church and Joseph gave a large donation from his personal savings without the blink of an eye, Cassandra's eyes filled with tears and she admitted that she might have judged her son too harshly.

———

It was not difficult to persuade Vivian toward further education. But her chosen field was not nursing, as her father had long ago forecast. She chose instead to study the Arts.

"What do you plan to do with it?" asked Samuel.

"There are ever so many ways one can go," replied Vivian.

"You don't need 'ever-so-many-ways'," said her practical father. "You just need one."

Vivian's stubborn chin protruded. "I'll choose when I know more about the choices," she maintained, and Samuel nodded and they sent her off to Montreal to study the Arts. But it was awfully hard for Cassandra to let her go. The only comfort was knowing she would be under the protective wing of Cassandra's parents.

————

Samuel had been called away on an emergency one day in late November and Cassandra paced the kitchen floor, lifting the curtain to look out the window every now and then. Her eyes would always go to the sky. It looked as if a storm was brewing and Cassandra did not like the looks of it.

"Please, Father," she prayed. "Let him have time to make it home first."

But the darkness of evening closed in around them and still no Samuel.

Christina sensed her mother's uneasiness. "He'll see the storm coming and stay put," she tried to assure her mother.

"I do hope so," said Cassandra, running a nervous hand over her hair.

"Would you like me to go to meet him?" asked Thomas, now a strapping youth with wide shoulders and almost as big a grin.

"No," responded Cassandra quickly. "It would just be one more to worry about out in the weather."

"I'd go with him," offered Peter.

"No," said Cassandra firmly and paced to the window again.

The night had fallen and along with it had come the wind. It tore at the limbs of the trees in the yard, and lashed out at the drain pipes that extended to the rain barrel. The swing, now hanging unused in the yard, swung back and forth in dizzying arcs, now lifting this way, then flipping that, then crashing blindly into one of the side poles that suspended it. The gate creaked and strained against each new blast. Cassandra feared that it might be pulled from its hinges.

Then the snow came with swirling, obscuring gusts, completely blotting out the outside world when at its peak and then falling back to give the viewer a look at what it was burying in white. Cassandra could soon tell that even the children were worried, though none of them confessed to the fact.

She was nearly wild with concern when the newly installed phone rang once—and then again. It was their number.

Thomas was the one to answer it.

"Hello. Hello," he called. "Yes . . . I can't hear you." A pause. "I'm sorry, I can't hear." Another longer pause. Cassandra felt her whole inner self twist.

"Pa? Is that you? Yes. Yes."

"Let me talk to him—please," pleaded Cassandra and Thomas handed her the receiver.

"Samuel?" said Cassandra. "Where are you?"

The phone line sputtered and cracked. It seemed forever before Cassandra heard his voice.

"—here at Lawsons'," he was saying. "Think . . . stay . . . storm . . ." Cassandra could pick up only a word now and then.

"If you are safe, stay where you are!" she shouted into the mouthpiece, not realizing that her words probably were no clearer to Samuel than his were to her. "Just stay where you are. We are fine. Come home when the storm is over," she continued to shout to him over the crackling line.

"—go now," she heard Samuel say and then, "Good-night," and the snapping turned to a buzz.

Cassandra stepped back and hung up the receiver. Three pairs of eyes studied her face.

"He's safe—at Lawsons'," she explained even though she was sure they already had the information. She had to say the words for her own comfort. "He's fine. He'll stay there until the storm is over." She read the relief on their faces.

"We'd better get to bed. Thomas—bank the fire, please. Peter, make sure the door is fastened securely. That wind could rip off anything. Christina, move the water pail over here away from the window. It could freeze if it's left there."

And Cassandra scurried about the room, making things secure and ready for the night and the raging storm.

She slept fitfully. Again and again she awakened to listen to the wind howl around them. Off and on she would think that it had abated, and then another gust would come, shaking the windows and rattling the eaves trough. Every time she heard its fury she thanked God again that Samuel was safe, and tried to get back to sleep.

It was toward morning when a new sound roused her. At first she dismissed it as just another sound of the storm and then she knew it wasn't so. It sounded more like knocking than the hammering of the wind. Someone was pounding on their door.

She climbed from bed and reached to light the lamp. Her bedroom held a chill in spite of the banked fires. She fumbled with the matches and finally got the wick to catch flame. Then she hurriedly wrapped her woolen robe around her and hastened to the door. On the way she met Thomas. He, too, was carrying a lamp. He had already been to the door and was coming back to get her.

"It's Mr. Hick. His wife is having her baby. They want Pa."

Cassandra looked at the window. She couldn't see out into the darkness, but she could still hear the wind blowing.

"But he isn't here," Cassandra said unnecessarily to her son.

"I told him. He wants to talk to you."

Cassandra passed on to the kitchen. She found a nervous man pacing the floor and stopping now and then to rage at the storm and the darkness.

"Mr. Hick?" said Cassandra, thinking to herself that prayer might work much better than cursing.

He swung to face her.

"The baby's on the way," he said quickly. "We've got to get back to Esther."

"But the doctor isn't in," repeated Cassandra, setting her lamp on the kitchen table. "He has been storm-delayed at the Lawsons'."

"I know—yer boy told me—an' I'm sorry to be askin' you to go out in this weather but—"

"Me?" said Cassandra incredulously.

"We need to hurry—beggin' yer pardon."

"But I've never delivered a baby," blurted out Cassandra.

"You know a lot more about it than I do, ma'am," insisted the father-to-be, and Cassandra had to concede the point.

"I'll get dressed," she replied in a shaky voice and picked up the lamp to head back to her bedroom, forgetting that she was leaving the man in the dark.

"Mama," said Thomas, appearing again with his lamp in his hand, "surely you don't intend to go out on a night like this."

"What choice do I have?" replied Cassandra. "If it were me lying in that bed, I'd want someone, anyone, to come to me."

Thomas realized she was not to be swayed and he moved toward the kitchen, determined to have her coat and boots warmed by the fire before she slipped into them.

———

Cassandra felt that they would never fight their way through the tearing wind. Several times, Mr. Hick had to stop and take her arm, almost pulling her through the storm. The snow swirled around them, adding to the already knee-deep drifts that hindered their progress. Icy chips struck them in the face, stinging cheeks and chin cruelly. Wind pulled at her clothing, threatening to tear her coat from her body. Cassandra clung to her garment, vainly trying to keep its protective warmth wrapped securely around her.

It seemed as if they would never make the short trip through the snow-camouflaged streets of the little town to the house that Joseph had helped to build, but eventually they managed to stumble up the walk and fight their way through the door.

Cassandra was out of breath and slumped into a nearby chair, gasping for air while the sudden warmth of the building threatened to suffocate her.

A groan from the bedroom reminded her of the reason for her coming, and she stiffened and looked to Mr. Hick, who had already cast his coat aside and was reaching for the lamp on the table.

"She's in here," he said to Cassandra, and she knew that she must somehow find the strength to follow him. With a quick prayer for guidance, she forced herself back onto her feet and followed the man, dropping her coat on the floor somewhere along the short journey.

Cassandra knew very little about assisting a birthing, but she did judge, and correctly so, that the woman did not have much longer.

"Some clean linens," she told the man. "And warm towels or blankets for the baby. Place some of them on the oven door and warm them up. This is a cold night to be welcoming a little one."

The little bit of action seemed to settle her and she drew a few deep breaths and approached the woman.

"This your first?" she asked and the woman shook her head.

"I lost one," she answered, fear in her voice.

Cassandra felt her body shiver. She prayed that the woman would not lose another baby.

"We are going to do our best to make sure that you and your baby are fine," she said, and knew that it was the most she could promise.

"We? Is Doc here, too?" asked the woman.

"No," admitted Cassandra. "No, just me. But I—I never work alone. I—I—" Would the woman understand? she wondered. "I always ask God to be with me," she said evenly and the woman looked at her blankly and then nodded her head in understanding. Cassandra saw tears in her eyes, but she didn't know if it was from the pain of childbirth—or some other pain that troubled her more deeply.

———

A baby girl was born just as the clock on the bedroom mantel said eight. Cassandra waited for a moment, tied and cut the umbilical cord, bundled the little one in a warm blanket that her father held out, and hastened off with her to the warmth of the kitchen. She looked fine and Cassandra prayed that it might be so.

She wasn't sure just what to do next, but she remembered Samuel cleaning up each of her babies.

"Little one," she said to the complaining infant, "you don't have the best welcoming committee in the world. Oh, not that we aren't glad to see you—it's just that we don't know the proper rules of etiquette in welcoming the newborn. If only Samuel were here—"

But Samuel and his black bag were somewhere out there in the new day, waiting for the storm to release them. Cassandra did the best she could, bundled the small baby up warmly and passed her to her father while she went to attend the new mother.

"She's fine," Cassandra smiled. "I think she's going to look just like you."

The young woman was in tears.

Cassandra moved to smooth the hair back from the mother's face and look into her eyes.

"Are you all right?" she asked earnestly.

"I'm fine—now," the young woman answered.

"I think the storm has passed," went on Cassandra. "We

have nothing to worry about now, except for you to get some rest. Do you think you can do that?"

"I'm sure I can," replied Mrs. Hick. "I feel like I've done five laundries."

Cassandra smiled at her description of labor.

"I'll send Dr. Smith over to see you as soon as he gets home," she promised. "And if you should need me in the meantime, get a neighbor boy to come for me."

The woman nodded. She was already looking sleepy.

Cassandra left the room and went to the kitchen.

"She needs to rest now," she said to the father, who sat by the kitchen stove with the baby in his arms. "If the baby fusses, take her in to her mother. She might want to nurse. If she sleeps, let your wife sleep, too."

He nodded.

Cassandra pulled on her heavy boots and found her coat lying across a kitchen chair.

"I'll send my husband over to check on both of them as soon as he gets home," she said and he nodded again.

She was about to pass out into the cold morning air when he called softly after her, "Mrs. Doc?"

She turned to look at him.

"Thanks," he blurted. "Thanks more than I can say. It woulda killed her to lose another baby."

Cassandra nodded and closed the door tightly.

———

By the afternoon everyone in town seemed to have heard about the new baby. Virginia walked through the snow to see Cassandra.

"I hear you had quite a night," she said as she shrugged out of her coat and leaned to slip off her boots.

Cassandra just smiled.

"Did Doc get home yet?"

"He's over checking on the new baby now," said Cassandra.

"Well, from what everyone is saying, Doc couldn't have

done a better job himself," said Virginia.

"Don't tease," responded Cassandra. "I was scared to death."

She turned to the stove to push the teakettle over the heat for a cup of tea.

"I suppose you've heard what they're calling her," went on Virginia.

"No," admitted Cassandra. "They hadn't named her when I left."

"Cassandra," said Virginia smugly. "Cassandra Joy."

Chapter Twenty-one

Weddings

Vivian was the first of their children to marry.

"It seems that all she got out of her Arts course was a young professor," Samuel remarked as he read her glowing letter home, telling of her plans.

The wedding was to take place in Montreal. "In Grandmother's church," Vivian said. Samuel arranged for a young intern to come in and cover for him during his absence and took two weeks off to travel with the family.

"You can stay longer if you wish," he told Cassandra. "But I should get back."

Cassandra shook her head. She knew from her last trip back East that two weeks would be long enough.

The children were all excited about the trip. Christina fairly bubbled. She, of course, couldn't remember that long-ago trip, and her young brothers had never seen their Montreal grandparents. Cassandra regretted that they would not know their grandfather, as Henry P. Winston had been gone for almost a year.

The days on the train not only gave Samuel a much-needed rest, but also gave the family time to sit together and chat about many things.

"You would have liked your grandfather," Cassandra told her family. "He was an energetic, intelligent man. Always busy. Always doing." She might have added "always gone," but she didn't. Though she realized now that she had resented his constant absence when she was a child.

Samuel added to the conversation. "If it hadn't been for Dr. Henry P. Winston, my professor, your grandfather, I might never have made it into medicine."

Cassandra looked at Samuel as though she wished to challenge the statement.

"You stood in the top five of your class," she said quietly.

"In class work, yes. But Henry P., through avenues unbeknown to me, managed to find funding so that I could stay in school."

"I didn't know that," said Cassandra, a new respect for her father growing within her.

"He did it for a number of his students," Samuel said.

"His 'pets,' you mean," teased Cassandra. "I tell you truthfully, children, his students, his 'pets,' saw far more of him than his family did."

Cassandra still referred to her offspring as "children" and thought of them as such, even though the youngest, Peter, was now fifteen and seeing himself as quite adult. If they resented it, they did not say so. As Thomas put it, "I expect she'll still be calling us children when God takes her home," and the others had smiled at the thought.

"Tell us what Grandmother is like," begged Christina, and Cassandra began a long presentation of her mother, her Montreal home, and her growing up years. Even Thomas listened intently. Cassandra painted such a glowing picture that when she finally stopped for a breath, Peter asked openly, "What did you go west for?"

Cassandra looked up, startled by his sudden question, then smiled and reached to clasp Samuel's hand. "I met a young man," she said coyly, "and he was going west—no stopping him."

"Well, I'm glad you did, Pa," said Peter. They no longer referred to Samuel as Papa. "Too childish" was their assessment. Samuel did not argue. Cassandra guessed that he rather preferred "Pa." It had been the name he used for his own father.

"I can hardly wait to see Vivian," said Christina, changing the conversation.

"She'll likely be a snob now that she's lived in the East," put in Thomas.

"Where'd you ever get that idea?" asked Cassandra, turning quickly to confront her son.

He shrugged carelessly. "I dunno. Heard it around. Folks are always saying it."

"Well, just because folks are saying it doesn't make it so." Not all of Cassandra's bit of red-headed temper had been dealt with over the years. But she cooled more quickly, was more repentant, when her temper did flare. It always seemed to amuse Samuel, and at times Cassandra felt that he teased her just to provoke a response. He chuckled now and Cassandra flushed and checked her outburst.

"I—I can't abide sweeping statements that—that take everyone in with one big brush," said Cassandra, gesturing widely with her hand. "All Easterners or all Westerners, all English or all Spanish, all doctors or farmers. We are individuals. We can make our own choices—even though we might not be allowed to shape our circumstances. If I'm a snob—it's because I choose to be one—not because I was born and raised in the East."

"You're not a snob," Christina answered her mother.

Cassandra flashed her a look that might have said she wasn't getting the point; at the same time she thanked the girl with her eyes for her support.

"You—all of you," Cassandra went on, waving a hand to include all her children in her circle of concern, "your father and I have tried to raise you properly. We have taught you the laws of God, the rules of proper conduct, the etiquette of society—but in the end you make your own choices. You decide who and what you will be."

She stopped for a breath and went on.

"I thank God that you have all made the most important first choice. You have, at various ages, come to the place where you have recognized God for who He is and given your hearts and lives to Him. That big step has been taken." Cassandra paused briefly, remembering the times over the years when each child had made his or her individual decision to invite Jesus to cleanse a heart and be in charge of a young life. She was so thankful for each of those decisions. So thankful.

Then she continued. "But you will have many more choices to make in life. Many changes. Many seasons of growth. Your father and I might guide you—will still give our love and support—but in all honesty, you are now all— even you, Peter—adults and responsible for what you do with your lives. As your father and I have done our best for you and taught you the proper way to live, we will not accept the blame if you—if you make foolish decisions—and end up— end up—stupid—and poor—and—and sinful. The choice is yours. We've given you some proper tools for life, but you must do the work."

Cassandra leaned back in her seat and took a deep breath. She had delivered her sermonette to her children with a good deal of passion in each word. She felt Samuel's fingers tighten around hers.

"Whew!" said Peter, ducking exaggeratedly in the corner, "I don't quite know whether to celebrate or—or cower."

Joseph began to laugh and soon the whole family joined in. When they had enjoyed a good chuckle, Samuel brought them back to seriousness again.

"Your mother is quite right," he said in his usual calm way. "We love you dearly—each one of you. If you give us cause to be proud by what you do in life, it will be your own doing—not ours. We will grant you full credit. We can take you only so far—you must go on from there. We have every confidence that because you have allowed God to be with you and in you, your choices will be right. He will guide you when we no longer are there for you. Always remember that. Pray for His direction—and when He makes it known to you— don't argue with Him concerning it. Be in agreement with His will."

They had family prayer together as the Canadian Pacific Railroad car rambled its clanging way toward the East.

Later in life, Cassandra was often to recall that trip, counting it as one of her most treasured family memories.

———

Joseph was the next to marry. He picked a local girl, one whom Cassandra and Samuel were happy to welcome to the family. It was a community wedding in their own little church with so many in attendance that they couldn't all fit, and the pastor opened the windows so his voice would carry to those who clustered chairs closely around the outside.

After the ceremony the many well-wishers gathered together for a huge community pot-luck feast. Cassandra looked around the gathering of town and country folks and could tie many memories to faces before her.

They really are my people, she thought in a burst of nostalgia. *I belong here—so totally.*

At that moment Mrs. Clement moved toward her, stooped and aging but with sharp eyes glinting, teeth softly clicking.

"Mis' Doc," she said with her usual candor, "ya raised yerself one fine family. Ever'one of 'em. Done yerself proud." Then before Cassandra could even respond she went on. "'Course, they had 'em an advantage. Yer eastern manners with their pa's common sense."

Cassandra smiled. She felt that she had just been paid a wonderful and sincere compliment.

———

Joseph and his Annie took a brief honeymoon at Waterton Lake and settled in the community where Joseph continued to build—but now on his own. He seemed to have made some good choices—and Cassandra and Samuel were pleased.

———

Frequent letters from Vivian indicated that she was happy with her husband and home. Cassandra always laid the letters aside with grateful feelings washing through her.

It was hard for her to wait to share the letters with Samuel. They always discussed the "happenings" after he'd had his chance to read.

As the months passed, Cassandra realized that the letters had taken a new turn. Vivian had learned to love her Grandmother Winston dearly, but she was now expressing increasing concern for the elderly woman's spiritual condition.

"I'm not sure that Grandmother really knows she has eternal life," she wrote in one such letter. "It worries me. She talks of church and good deeds as though that is what will gain her entrance to heaven. I have tried to explain, but so far she doesn't seem to understand. Please pray for me."

Cassandra's eyes filled with tears as she remembered the times she had tried in her own letters to explain the difference to her mother and father. Her attempts had fallen on deaf ears as well.

"Perhaps Vivian will have more success," she said to Samuel after he had read the letter. He nodded. They joined hands and prayed together.

———

Christina went off to the city. She didn't wish to continue her education immediately, she said. She didn't know if she wished to go on to school at all. What she did want to do was to become a telephone operator—so that is exactly what she did, and loved it.

"At least there is one advantage," said Samuel. "She can call as often and for as long as she likes, and it won't cost us anything."

But the telephone company didn't see it quite that way, so Christina told them to call her because she "was saving money." Their telephone bills reflected the fact that they had a daughter in Lethbridge.

———

Thomas was the next to marry. He seemed so young to

Cassandra. Only twenty. But he had completely made up his mind and there seemed to be no dissuading him.

He had chosen a lovely young girl who worked at a Calgary law office while Thomas was finishing his classes to be a pharmacist. They settled in Calgary and Beth quit her job and cheerfully went home to be a housekeeper, wife, and, she added with a twinkle in her eyes, prospective mother.

————

Christina met her chosen at a church in Lethbridge. He was a young pastor on his first assignment. It didn't take the young people long to decide that their lives should be joined together. Samuel and Cassandra, along with Joseph, Annie and Peter, made the trip to Lethbridge for the wedding. Thomas and Beth came from Calgary. Vivian sent her regrets. She was expecting their first child in a month's time and didn't dare risk the trip. "Just in case," she explained.

"What's the matter?" teased Samuel in a telephone conversation. "Don't you trust your father? I have delivered half of the population here at Jaret—including you."

But in serious moments, even Samuel agreed that it would not be wise for Vivian to make the long, tiring trip.

The wedding was lovely and Samuel and Cassandra took to their new son instantly.

"Rev. and Mrs. George Dawson," announced the officiating pastor, and Christina and George turned to the audience with matching smiles. As they walked the aisle together as husband and wife, Christina threw kisses to Cassandra and Samuel.

————

Vivian gave birth to a baby boy. It was all Cassandra could do to keep from boarding the first train back to Montreal. Samuel had promised her that they would make the trip together in June. That was months away. The baby would be four months old before she even got to hold him.

But Cassandra held herself in check. If she went immediately, there was the chance that Samuel would cancel his plans to make the trip. She knew Vivian was just as anxious to show off her new son to her father as she was to her mother. Cassandra decided she would make herself wait until June.

They named the baby Samuel Henry, and Cassandra couldn't hold back the tears that slipped out from under her lashes.

————

Peter seemed reluctant to leave home. When asked his plans for the future, he replied with a shrug, "I dunno yet. I'm still thinking about it—and praying too."

"I hope you are prepared to have that boy underfoot when he's fifty," Samuel smiled one day as he and Cassandra breakfasted together.

Cassandra sipped slowly from her steaming cup of coffee.

"He doesn't seem in a hurry, does he?" she responded.

"I'm glad he at least has work," Samuel commented.

Peter was working with Joseph, building a new business block in downtown Jaret.

But when Peter did finally make up his mind, he surprised them both.

"I want to be a doctor," he informed them one night. "I have prayed about it for a long time and I feel sure that God is urging me in that direction."

Samuel and Cassandra exchanged smiles.

"And then I am applying to the mission board," went on Peter. "I feel God is calling me to medical work in Africa, possibly Nigeria."

The smiles disappeared. Concern first flashed across two faces, and then pride and joy brought tears to their eyes. Samuel reached out his hand and took the strong, already calloused hand of his son, while Cassandra fought to keep the tears from falling.

"We'll do all we can to support you," said Samuel, his voice a bit husky.

"I know you will, Pa," replied the young man. "You always have."

————————

Cassandra felt that she had prepared herself for the leaving of her youngest. After all, he was no longer a child. He was a man. But deep down in her heart she knew he would always be her little boy—her baby. She choked back sobs and held him for a long time. She didn't say, "I'll miss you," but she knew he got her message. Besides, she couldn't get the words past the lump in her throat.

They were proud of him as they watched him climb aboard the outgoing train. But he would be such a long, long way from them. And she was going to feel so alone with the last one gone from home.

She and Samuel drove the many miles home from Calgary alone. The trip went faster now. The Model T shortened the hours on the roads. Cassandra still watched the skies for thunderstorms. She knew what could happen to the roads if the rain fell too heavily.

"It's going to seem different," she mused to Samuel.

He kept his eyes on the road. Cassandra guessed that he was fighting his emotions just as much as she.

He nodded his head, his jaw set.

When he did finally speak, his words surprised her— though they shouldn't have. "They're all good kids," he said with deep feeling. "Every one of them."

Chapter Twenty-two

The March of Time

The house seemed too big. Cassandra didn't know what to do with all the spare room—or the spare time. Neighborhood children helped fill in the time factor to some degree. They still came with their skinned knees, their slivers, and their small cuts and asked her to care for them.

They also brought their little animals. Cats with torn ears, dogs with porcupine quills, rabbits with scratched noses. Cassandra doctored them all as best she could. She made sure she had simple medicines and plenty of bandages on hand and even took to discussing her animal cases with Samuel to ensure she wasn't doing something wrong or missing something.

"I'm not a veterinarian," he would tell her, "but it sounds about right. Don't know of anyone around who could do any more."

Word traveled. Eventually local farmers stopped her on the street to ask about a horse with a lame leg or a cow with a split udder. Cassandra felt uncomfortable at times, but she advised as best she could.

But even with her "doctoring," her days seemed to hang heavily on her hands. One day as she sat on the back porch shelling fresh peas from her garden, Samuel came up the walk. He had just returned from a house call in the country and knew that his office would be full of patients waiting for his attention. *Already he looks tired,* thought Cassandra, and she hurried to fix him a cup of tea.

As he sipped it slowly, he seemed to be in deep thought.

"What would you think of helping out in the office again?" he asked her at last.

Her head came up quickly. Had she been missing something?

"Aren't you feeling well?" she asked.

"Oh, I'm fine. Fine. But I don't have the drive I used to. Thought that with the two of us working together, I might not have to put in such long days."

Cassandra popped another peapod, her eyes on the bowl in her lap. Relieved that Samuel was all right, she nodded slowly.

"Don't see why not," she answered Samuel. "My household chores sure don't take all my time anymore."

Samuel grinned. He knew it was hard for her to be without children in the house and that time hung heavy for her.

The arrangement was made. She went to the office for two hours each morning and again in the afternoon for as long as Samuel needed her. It seemed to work out just fine.

———

Cassandra decided that the grandchildren came in bunches. Vivian added a girl at about the same time that Joseph and Ann had their first, also a girl. Then in another two years, Christina and George had a boy and Thomas and Beth had a girl. Two years following, Vivian gave birth to another girl, Christina and Joseph both had boys. And in another three years it was a boy for Joseph, and a girl for Christina and for Thomas. In a matter of a dozen years, they were grandparents to ten grandchildren. And yet, except for Joseph's three, all of them were many miles away. Cassandra wished they all could be near.

But Joseph's Sallie Jo and Adam were a great joy to their grandparents and spent as much time as possible at the house. The old swing in the yard had to be repaired, and the sandbox was filled with fresh sand.

Samuel even bought some new toys, since trucks and cars were now all the rage rather than the wagons their own children had played with.

Sallie Jo was a dainty little girl, full of energy and intriguing questions.

"Why do geese fly like that?"

Her grandfather studied the vee in the sky and tried to explain simply.

"If it works like that, why didn't God tell the other birds?" she wanted to know.

Grandfather had no answer to that question.

Sallie Jo studied the geese for a moment longer and then asked again, "Who chooses the leader? Do they have a 'lection?"

Cassandra smiled, wondering how Samuel was going to answer that one.

"You know," he said. "I've heard that they don't have just one leader. They work well together. One takes the lead—we'll say it's a big gander—though it might not be, but it has to be a big strong bird to lead the way through the sky. Then when his wings begin to tire, another goose moves in and takes his place and he drops back into the vee where it isn't quite as hard bucking the air current and rests a bit as he flies. Then another might take the lead for a while—and another."

Sallie Jo gazed upward at the geese. They were disappearing in the afternoon haze.

"Sort of like in church, huh?" she commented and her grandfather frowned slightly.

"We change leaders too. You told us about Pastor Ray getting old and tired so now Pastor Shriver is here. When he gets tired, someone else will come. And in Sunday school, Mrs. Peters isn't gonna teach anymore. I heard her say to Mrs. Walters, 'Let the younger set take over. I've had my turn.'"

Samuel smiled at the granddaughter he called Pixie and ran his hand over her head of brown curly hair.

Sallie Jo looked steadfastly at her grandfather, hazel eyes so much like Samuel's.

"But one shouldn't fall back into the vee until you really need a rest, should you?" she added solemnly. "That would be quitting too soon."

"Right," he said, nodding vigorously. "Right. One shouldn't quit too soon. Just like the geese."

Cassandra wondered if the small girl didn't have more sense than many adults.

———

Every letter from Peter in faraway Africa brought them information on the needs of the people. Cassandra knew that Joseph and Ann gave as generously to the support of the mission's medical work as she and Samuel did.

But the letter she was holding in her hand held more than just a report on needs of the small clinic. Cassandra's eyes opened wide and her heart began to beat foolishly as she read his words.

"I have met a nurse," he began. "She works with the same mission right here in our little hospital. She is from the U.S., Michigan, in fact, and, Mama, you would approve of her. She's wonderfully sensitive and caring. She loves the Lord and is careful to ask for His guidance before she leaps in and makes decisions—and besides all that—she has lovely blue eyes and a wonderful smile."

"Oh, God," breathed Cassandra, hugging the letter to her heart. "You know how I have prayed for a good companion for Peter. Perhaps this is your answer to my prayers."

She turned her attention back to the letter.

"We have been seeing a good deal of each other. Our work really doesn't leave us much time for socializing; but when we do have some free time, we go for walks or just sit in the cool of the hospital veranda and chat. This usually doesn't happen until after the sun goes down because of our long days, so it can actually be cool at times.

"We haven't made any definite plans as yet, but I am

seriously considering making some. It would be so wonderful to have a dedicated mate—both a work-mate and a soul-mate. She is really very special."

Cassandra could not wait for Samuel to come home. She removed her apron, tucked the letter into her dress pocket, hurriedly pinned on her bonnet and rushed off down the board sidewalk to his office. She knew he would be as excited as she was.

————

Samuel and Cassandra continued working side by side in the little office and came home at night to the serenity of their small home. As the years passed, they were no longer on the edge of the town. It had grown up all around them until they were in the middle of any hustle and bustle the small town could boast.

With greater frequency, Samuel brought in a young doctor to care for the practice while the Smiths took two or three weeks to go visit with their grandchildren. That way they were able to more or less keep up with the happenings in the lives of their offspring.

Peter did marry his Rachel. Cassandra was so thankful that Peter was no longer without human companionship. "I know that God was present with you," she wrote, "but it is so nice to know that you have Rachel's presence as well."

Cassandra and Samuel did not get to meet her until the couple came home on furlough. They heartily agreed with his assessment of his helpmate and were open in telling him so.

Peter smiled and put his arm around Rachel's waist, drawing her close.

"And we are to have our first child," he informed them, "next June."

Cassandra Elaine was born on June 26. Wonderfully hale and hearty—and many, many miles away from her grandparents on the other side of the world.

————

Peter and Rachel added two boys to their family, and Vivian, after thinking for ten years that their family was complete, had another boy as well. That gave Cassandra and Samuel a total of fourteen grandchildren.

"That is enough!" said Samuel in mock consternation, and Cassandra smiled. None of their children had reached the number of five—as she and Samuel had.

Even so, Cassandra was willing to agree with Samuel. Fourteen was enough. The older ones were all set to graduate from high school and were already making plans as to what they wished to do in life. Daily Cassandra and Samuel prayed that God would be allowed to give them His guidance.

————

Cassandra didn't feel comfortable driving the car, so Samuel had hitched the horse to the buggy. He still kept horses. There were many times when a car would not have gotten him to the farmhouse where he was needed.

He preferred the car, but when the weather was uncooperative and the mud or snowdrifts deep on the prairie roads, he knew he could still count on his horses to get him through.

But Cassandra drove the buggy as much for enjoyment as for necessity. She loved the feel. Loved the air. Loved the quiet. Loved the solitude. So when arrangements were made for her to travel out to see Mrs. Fleming to change the dressing on her leg, Samuel did not even need to ask if she preferred taking the buggy. He hitched the trustworthy bay rather than the spirited black and brought the buggy to their hitching rail.

"I'll be home in plenty of time to prepare your supper," Cassandra informed him and kissed him on the cheek.

The shock of hair that still slipped over his forehead was silver-gray now. Cassandra found it just as attractive as when he had been a young man. She raised a hand to run her fingers through the hair, a bit thinner now but not a lot, and pushed it back into place.

"Take your time," he said to her, knowing how much she enjoyed short drives in the country.

———

She changed the dressing on the leg, concerned that the sore was not healing as it should be, then washed her hands and joined Mrs. Fleming at her kitchen table. They were new people to the area and Cassandra felt they needed to be shown special friendship while they got acquainted with new neighbors.

They sipped coffee, though Cassandra had never tasted such bitter coffee, and chatted. The woman seemed hungry for companionship and Cassandra kept one eye on the clock, knowing that she should be on her way home but reluctant to leave until the woman had enjoyed a good visit.

I must come more often, she thought as she finally excused herself.

The woman walked with her to the buggy, still talking, still unable to say her goodbye. At last Cassandra had to take leave and the woman stood and waved until the buggy had left the lane and was back on the country road. Cassandra saw her wave one last time, turn and walk toward her house, limping slightly on the troublesome leg.

"She does need company," Cassandra mused. "Poor soul. I must tell Virginia. She has more time for neighborhood calls then I do and is awfully good about taking in a cake or some cookies. I'm sure she'd go."

Cassandra looked at the sky. It was late in the afternoon. She was late. Samuel would surely beat her home. He'd be wondering where his supper was long before she returned.

She pushed the mare, coaxing her into a brisk trot. The road was rutted and the buggy bounced, but Cassandra braced herself and clucked to the mare again.

She was almost to the edge of town when the accident happened. If she had not been so preoccupied with hurrying home, she likely would have seen the covey of partridges. But she was concerned about Samuel's late supper. The mare didn't seem to notice the birds either. Not until there was a whirring of wings and a splash of color and movement as the whole flock lifted at the same time and seemed to spin into multiple directions.

Before Cassandra had time to react, the mare bolted. Her hands had been holding the reins loosely, so she was unable to gain quick control. Before she knew it the buggy was bouncing down and across the ditch and then she felt it going over. There was nothing to cling to but the reins, and of course they gave her no support. She fell heavily, hitting the hard-packed earth with her hip and elbow. She felt a searing pain surge through her at the same time she heard the frightened whinny of the mare and the buggy smack against the ground and pieces splintering all around her.

And then something hit her head with a dull thud and all went black. Cassandra lay where she had fallen. She heard the story of the accident later, piece by piece, from one person or another during her days of recovery.

The mare, after freeing herself of most of the buggy parts, continued on home in a frantic state, dragging bits of buggy tongue and harness along with her. It was Mr. Hick who caught up to her in the street. He managed to quiet her and release her from some of the pieces that had her spooked. Then he hurried down the street to the doctor's house. He expected to meet Cassandra and hated to inform her that Doc must have had an accident or the mare had broken loose from some hitching rail.

But it was Samuel who met him on the porch.

"This yer horse, ain't she?" said Mr. Hick.

Samuel took one look and said under his breath, "Oh, dear God. Red has had an accident."

He didn't bother to grab his coat. Just jumped in his new Ford and started down the road toward the Flemings. He had left the town before he realized that Mr. Hick was in the car beside him.

"Now, hold on, Doc," the man was saying. "Horse might have just broken tether."

It was possible. Samuel knew that it was possible and he prayed with all his heart that it might be so.

But they had not gone far before they spotted the broken bulk of the buggy in the ditch. Doc pulled the Ford over to the side of the road and fairly jumped from the rolling vehicle.

They found her there, crumpled and unconscious. They lifted her gently, and tenderly transported her back to town.

Samuel stayed with her day and night. On the third day she stirred, opened her eyes and looked at him in confusion.

"You had a little mishap," he said in answer to her unasked question.

"What happened?"

"I'm not sure. Old Bert ditched you for some reason."

Cassandra frowned again. There was something in the back of her mind. If she could only— She was sure that the secret was locked there, if she could—

"Don't worry about it now," said Samuel. "It'll all sort itself out in time. It's good to see you awake. How do you feel?"

Cassandra tried to take stock of her body. Everything seemed to ache and nothing seemed to work.

"You tell me," she answered him candidly. "You're the doctor."

Samuel waited for a moment and then replied truthfully, "You got a pretty good shaking. Bruised an arm and broke your hip. They'll mend. It was your head I was worried about."

She lifted her good hand and then cried in alarm, "Samuel. You've shaved off all my hair!"

"Had to," he apologized. "Had to see where you got hit."

He paused and let his gaze drop to his hands that slowly clasped and unclasped as he held them before him, his elbows leaning on his outspread knees. At length he cleared his throat and lifted shadowed eyes to gaze directly into her green ones.

"It was one of the hardest things I've ever done," he confessed. "Like taking off an arm—or a leg."

Cassandra knew his anguish and ached for him. At the same time she felt her own loss. For the first time in her entire life, she would have loved to have her head covered with her own red hair. Any color would have been preferred to no hair at all.

She let her hand drop. She didn't know whether to weep or to laugh.

Oh, dear God, she prayed quickly and then turned to Samuel. "I must be a sight," she said with emphasis.

He leaned over and kissed her. "You are beautiful," he said.

Then he straightened and his eyes took on a teasing glow. "You know—I believe it emphasizes your green eyes."

"Oh, get—" cried Cassandra, and then began to chuckle softly.

What did it really matter? It was getting to be more gray than red anyway.

————

During her long days of convalescence Cassandra had more callers than she could count. Virginia fashioned a lacy bonnet for her head, "So I won't scare away any visitors," Cassandra told her wryly. Women came with pies and cakes and stews and fried chicken. There was so much food in the house that Doc had to call a halt, and Virginia wisely organized the carry-ins so that the Smiths were supplied without having excess piling up in the icebox and pantry.

Children came—just to chat or to entertain her with one of their pets.

Even the menfolk came, keeping her posted about the new calves, the state of the crop, or the danger of early frost to her rose bushes.

Sallie Jo and Adam called almost daily and Cassandra loved their visits. They were really getting quite grown up and could be a good help, as well as good company.

Cards and letters came frequently from other family members. Christina and George drove up a number of times from Lethbridge and Thomas and Ann came down from Calgary. Vivian could not come and it bothered her. She called often on the phone and begged her mother to take her time in recovering and then to take the train to Montreal and spend some days of recuperation with her.

Peter wrote, feeling far away and helpless to give any aid to the family in their trying circumstance.

But true to Samuel's word, she did heal. And her hair even began to grow back in. At first it seemed fine and fuzzy. Almost like a baby's head. But it thickened and gained more body, and Cassandra was pleased that she would soon be able to lay aside her cloth bonnet and let her hair be her natural covering.

"Well, I guess God answered my prayer," Cassandra remarked dryly to Virginia one day.

When Virginia asked which prayer, Cassandra said, "You don't know how many hours I spent asking Him to change the color of my hair when I was a child. Well, He has. Though it does seem a bit late."

Virginia smiled.

Rather than a heavy head of red-turning-gray hair, Cassandra now had short, slightly curling soft white hair.

"It's pretty, actually," said Virginia. "It becomes you."

Cassandra nodded. "I know," she said with a smile, mimicking Samuel's teasing. "It emphasizes my green eyes."

Chapter Twenty-three

Life Goes On

It was almost two years before Cassandra felt that her hip was working properly again. Even then it would cause her a few twinges when the weather changed or when she was on her feet for too long at a stretch.

But she was thankful to have full use of her limbs and began to plan another spring garden. Her children all cautioned her not to overdo it and she promised them, one by one, that she would be careful.

It was still hard for her to believe that she and Samuel now had married grandchildren.

"Before we know it, we'll be great-grandparents," Samuel remarked one day as they closed the door to his office. "No wonder I have less energy than I used to have."

"I haven't noticed you slowing down any," countered Cassandra. He still worked far too hard. The children were constantly begging him to retire, but he shook his head.

"I haven't heard of a younger man who wants my practice," he would say. "The people in Jaret still have tummy aches and broken bones. They need a doctor—and I need something to do with my time. There never was a good fishing hole around here."

No fishing hole. No young grandchildren. Even Adam had grown and left him. Cassandra really didn't blame Samuel for wanting to keep his hours filled. She didn't know what he would do if he didn't have his practice.

"It's different for a woman," she said to Virginia as they sat at tea one day. Virginia now had difficulty holding her cup properly, for arthritis had twisted her fingers, but they still took tea together on the front porch whenever Virginia could join her.

"Women always have their work," Cassandra went on. "The cooking, the cleaning, the many household chores. Even if I stopped going down to the office, I could still fill my days. Especially now that I don't move as fast anymore."

Virginia laughed. "I find I've gotten so slow that my days aren't long enough to do the necessary chores," she admitted.

"But for our menfolk," continued Cassandra, "quitting work is a whole change of life. I don't think Samuel would be happy—I really don't."

"No," said Virginia, struggling with both hands to get her cup to her lips, "Morris wouldn't be either."

"He still goes in every day?"

"Every day but Sunday," replied Virginia, then added with a chuckle, "And I am thankful. Can't imagine how it would be to have him at my elbow all day. He'd be bored—and I'd be crazy."

They both laughed, then changed the subject to bring each other up-to-date on the latest events among their family members.

"I almost hate the thought of going to Montreal," Cassandra said to Samuel. They were packed and ticketed, heading for another grandchild's wedding, but this was the first trip that they had taken to the East for some time.

Samuel took her arm to assist her up the steep steps to the Pullman. "Why?" he asked innocently. "You know Vivian is counting on us—but if you'd rather not go—"

"Oh, I wouldn't think of backing out," hastened Cassandra. "She'd be sure to jump to the conclusion that I wasn't feeling well or something."

"And you are?" asked Samuel. He had continued to be concerned ever since her accident, even though she had many times assured him that she was fine.

"I'm fine," she said again and gave the words a bit of a punch.

He chuckled. "Well, you still have your spunk, anyway. I'm glad for that."

They found their seat and settled for the long ride. Cassandra was glad that they would not need to be sitting the whole time but could retire to berths as soon as the train was on its way.

"What were you saying about Montreal?" Samuel reminded her.

"What about Montreal?" asked Cassandra. Things seemed to slip her mind more easily than they had in the past. She often wondered if it was because of the bump on the head.

"You said that you almost hated to go there," Samuel reminded her.

"Oh yes. That. Nothing much, I guess. Just a feeling. It'll seem strange with Mama gone and the old house sold, that's all."

Samuel nodded.

Cassandra knew it would be difficult. Her mother had passed away while she'd been bedridden with her hip, so she hadn't been able to go to the funeral. But she did thank God with her whole being that Vivian, with God's help, had finally been able to get her mother to understand that she needed to prepare herself for death and heaven. A few days before she had died, she had done just that—asking God, in Jesus' name, to accept her as His child.

"Well—it will be nice to see Vivian—and the family," said Cassandra. She knew that would give the trip meaning.

"This is her last. Her little tag-along," commented Samuel. "Things will be changing for her as well."

Cassandra's eyes clouded. She knew how Vivian would be feeling. She felt that she knew all about change. She had experienced a few changes of her own. Without thinking she raised a hand to gently ease her silver hair under the brim of her new navy hat. She thought the hat quite becoming—especially as it contrasted with her white hair.

"Yes," she mused. "Yes—changes do come. Sometimes gently—sometimes harshly. But they do come."

"What was the hardest of life's changes for you, Red?" Samuel asked, curling his fingers around her hand. He still called her "Red" even though there wasn't a bit of red to her hair anymore. She supposed it was just habit—but she had grown to like his pet name.

"I don't really know," she answered slowly. "Guess the hardest was going west."

He looked surprised at her admission.

"That was hard?" he asked.

She smiled at him and shifted her hand so she could wrap her fingers around his also.

"You'll never know how hard," she answered honestly.

"I *didn't* know," he said and seemed surprised that he hadn't understood.

"You were much too busy to see it. First the house. Then the practice. Then children—building—patients—you were a busy man."

"Well, I shouldn't have been that busy," he admitted. Then he continued softly. "I don't suppose it's coming at the right time—but I'm sorry, Red. Really sorry. I had no idea you were finding it so tough—but I should have been more—more sensitive."

"I got over it," she sighed. "Virginia did it for me. Virginia—and finding God."

"I remember," he said, toying with her hand. "I was so surprised when you told me you hadn't known God all along. I couldn't believe it. I mean—I had no plans to marry a woman who didn't know God." He waited for a few moments, drawing a meaningless pattern on her palm with his finger. "And I was so busy being a doctor that I didn't catch that either. I'm sorry."

"I thought I did know Him. If you would have asked me, I would have answered, thinking I was being perfectly honest, 'Yes, I know Him.' I didn't know the difference between knowing about Him and knowing Him personally." She let her thoughts drift for a moment, then pulled them back. "Well, I do now."

"Yes," he said. "Thanks to Virginia." Then he sighed and leaned back in the seat. "That was a long time ago," he reminded her.

"Yes, a long time ago," she agreed.

What was there about long train rides that made her get so philosophical? Maybe it was simply because one had to take the time to sit and think. There was nothing else to be done. Perhaps the train ride would be good for her, after all. Perhaps it would be good for both of them. They had been together almost constantly for many years—and yet there was never time to really sit and reflect—to talk about thoughts and feelings and—growing. Cassandra changed her mind about the trip. She was glad they had this time to be together—just the two of them.

———

They had been home for only four days and were just getting back into the swing of things when Cassandra's whole world changed. A change that she had not counted on. The hardest change of her life.

She was at the cupboard doing up the breakfast dishes before going down to the office when there was a loud pounding on her door.

"Mrs. Doc, yer to come quick," gasped young Will Moore when she answered.

"What's wrong?" she asked him, fear gripping her.

"I dunno," the boy replied. "I was jest told to get you on the double."

He was panting hard so Cassandra was sure he must have followed orders.

There must be some emergency, said Cassandra to herself. *Samuel wouldn't call me away from my kitchen chores unless he needed me badly.*

She didn't stop for her shawl. The day was mild. She didn't even stop for her hat. It was one of only a few times that she had left her house without her hat firmly in place.

She would have walked right out and left the back door open had not Will noticed and stepped forward to close it behind her.

He took her arm solicitously and she allowed him to help her hurry down the newly poured concrete sidewalk.

When they reached the office there was a good deal of commotion. Cassandra was prepared to push her way through but as she neared the throng, folks fell back, allowing her passage.

"What is it?" she asked Morris when she spotted him near the door to the inner office. "An emergency?"

Morris nodded and took her arm. They had grown old together, the two couples. He knew her about as well as anyone in the town—except for his Virginia.

When he opened the door, Cassandra was surprised to see Virginia standing there, her eyes already red from weeping—her twisted hand extended out to her. It all seemed so strange. She couldn't understand.

Out of the corner of her eye she saw a form lying on the cot in the corner, but Samuel was not there bending over the patient as Cassandra expected him to be.

"Where's Samuel?" she heard herself asking and then Virginia stepped back, her hand on Cassandra's arm, and indicated the corner cot.

Samuel was lying there, his face washed of color. His hands were folded on his chest.

"What happened?" Cassandra managed to gasp, but she still didn't understand.

She pulled away from Virginia so that she might go to him. He needed her. He looked so pale. He must be ill.

But Morris held her arm firmly. "He's gone, Cassandra," he said quietly but firmly. "He's gone. It was his heart."

What was he saying? Her head whirled in confusion.

Again Morris spoke the words, "He's gone."

It hit her then but she still refused to believe him. She

fought against the truth with all her being. "He can't be," she insisted. "He just left home an hour ago. He was fine. It can't be."

Morris let her go then, though both he and Virginia stayed by her side. She crossed to Samuel and knelt by his lifeless body. At first she could not weep. She could not even feel. She thought that time must have stopped. That she was suspended in empty space, whirling in dizzying confusion—or having some horrid dream. There seemed to be no reality anymore.

She reached out a hand and brushed back the lock of silver hair. Yes. Yes. It was Samuel. Her Samuel. She had lost him. He was gone and she was left alone. And she hadn't even had a chance to say goodbye.

She wept then. She laid her head against his silent heart and wept until she had no more tears.

———

All the children except Peter came home for the funeral. Most of the grandchildren were able to come as well. They made quite a group as they clung together, smiling as they greeted one another through their tears. Cassandra let her eyes pass from one to another, and in spite of her heavy heart, she felt joy.

He was so proud of them all, she remembered and was glad that none of them had ever let him down.

They had to hold the funeral service out-of-doors. People came from miles away. The people he had tended, had sat up with through long nights of illness, had mended and stitched and coaxed to life or back to life. Cassandra had never seen such a crowd. Over and over again she heard the words: "I'm so sorry, Mrs. Doc. He was a good man."

Yes, he was a good man—but she hated the past tense. For her he would always be a good man, one she carried with her in her heart wherever she went.

———

They took her home and made her tea and fussed over and pampered her. She was grateful. She needed their love and their supportive hugs, but she still felt empty—dead and empty. She wasn't sure they understood just how much of herself she had lost.

"What are you planning to do now, Mama?" She had known the question would come. Had been dreading it. She hoped with all her heart that they didn't push for some kind of change before she had a chance to sort things out—get back some kind of reality—make some sort of sense out of her world. She acted innocent.

"What do you mean?" she said.

"You can't stay here," said Christina.

"I've been here all my life," she replied.

"But—not on your own. We can't just leave you here on your own."

"Why don't you come home to Montreal?" asked Vivian.

Cassandra knew they meant well. Knew they loved her. But she also knew she had no intention of going to Montreal. She'd never be able to stand it.

She shook her head.

"I—I don't think I'd fit in there anymore." That was all she was able to say.

"But you'd learn to fit in again. I did," insisted Vivian.

But you were a child, Cassandra wished to say. *You were looking for adventure—love. And you found it. What am I to look for? I want neither. I want—I just want my friends—my memories—a chance to feel alive again.*

But Cassandra did not voice any of her thoughts. She was sure her family would not understand.

"I'll move back," said Joseph at her side. He had moved his family from the small town seven years before and was now building houses in the city. "A small town can grow only so far," he had explained at the time of the move. "We are about as big as we can get. I need to move elsewhere if I am to find steady work."

Cassandra and Samuel had not argued. They knew that Joseph was right, but at the time it had been a bit hard for them to let their last family members move away from them.

But they had managed. Had soon made the adjustment. Samuel had even teased about it. "Now we have no one looking over our shoulder, Red," he had said. "We can finally be our own boss."

But they had missed Joseph and Ann, just as they had missed Sallie Jo and Adam when they had grown up and left the small town.

Now Joseph, who was considering his own retirement, was gently and unselfishly offering to move back so that his mother would not be alone.

She managed to pat his hand and give him a smile, but she shook her head. "No. No," she said firmly. "It isn't at all necessary. I wouldn't want you to do that."

"But you need someone—," began Christina again.

"My lands!" she exclaimed, a bit of her old fire returning. "I have a whole town full of folk."

"But—"

"Mother's right," cut in Thomas. "She needs some time to sort things out. If she's happiest here, then I think she should stay. At least until . . ." He didn't finish his statement. He didn't say "until she can no longer care for herself," but the words seemed to hang all around them.

At least he had bought her some time. She was grateful for that and she reached out to squeeze his hand.

———

They finally left her alone. She watched them go. One carload after another, and when the final ones were gone she sat down at the kitchen table and had a good cry.

She felt drained. Completely empty. She didn't even hurt—she felt so dead inside. She wondered if she would ever feel alive again. She could not have counted the number of funerals she had attended over the years. A number of them had been patients that skill and medicine had failed to save. But never had she realized what it was to be left the living dead. Did others feel as she did? Had her mama, when her papa had passed away? She hadn't known. Hadn't even guessed. Had been totally unable to offer the right kind of understanding.

Cassandra pulled herself up from her chair and went to undress. The bedroom seemed still—cold—lifeless. She supposed she would have to get used to the emptiness. But it was not going to be easy.

Chapter Twenty-four

Starting Over

She wasn't sure how it all happened, but the days slowly slipped by with the routine of living. Another winter came and went, they moved on to spring, and soon her garden was growing again.

Virginia had been her mainstay. There was hardly a day that she didn't drop by. As their custom had been over the years when the weather was nice, they took their tea on the front porch. Cassandra's roses bloomed in the front bushes.

Her children wrote and phoned and came to call. She appreciated their solicitude—but she still felt lonely.

Her pain had been even more intense as the initial numbness began to leave. She had thought for a few terrible weeks that she wouldn't be able to bear it. But everyone had been so kind and Virginia had always been there for the worst days, and gradually—oh so gradually—the pain began to lessen just a little.

———

One summer day as she knelt over a flower bed she heard young feet running over the sidewalk again and looked up to see little Cassandra Grey, one of her namesakes. *It is so good to see a child in my yard again,* she thought, and smiled warmly.

"Hello, Cassandra."

But the girl responded with excited, breathless words. "Mrs. Doc—Herbie hurt his foot."

It had been some time since a child had called her Mrs. Doc—had called on her for help.

"Where is he?" she asked, pushing herself up from her crouching position with some difficulty. Samuel would have fretted if he had seen her. Her old hip injury gave her a bit of trouble at times.

"He's over by the new 'struction," said the little girl and reached for Cassandra's hand.

Cassandra willingly clasped the small hand in hers and went along with her to see the boy.

She could hear his crying before they arrived. There he was, curled up on the ground, his foot thrust out before him. It didn't take long for Cassandra to spot the problem. He had stepped on a sharp piece of wood with his bare foot.

She had to carry him home. Her arms were tired and she was puffing from the exertion by the time she reached her gate, but she made it.

She lowered him to her kitchen table and got out Samuel's black bag that had been stored for many months unused in the hall closet. She was glad that she knew what to do. How to remove the intruding item. How to properly disinfect and bandage. By the time she had the job done the boy's tears were gone and small Cassandra was quite impressed with big Cassandra's work.

From then on, her little patients came to her again. There was no other place to go. The town had not yet been successful in obtaining another doctor.

At first Cassandra had not cared that Samuel had not been replaced. She was still hurting too much to think of others. Then she had reasoned that it was "proper," that no one else really could take Samuel's place. It was fitting that his office doors should remain closed. But as the days passed and she began to heal within and also to notice the needs of the town, she upbraided herself for her selfish negligence and began to spend long hours in letter writing, fighting to get another doctor for the small town and someone to take over Samuel's practice.

At last she found a candidate—but he wanted to drive out to see the town for himself. Businesslike, he also wanted to go over Samuel's books. Cassandra had no idea about the books. That was one department that Samuel had handled totally on his own.

But with the young doctor coming she decided that perhaps she should be prepared to show him the accounts. The day came when she picked up the office key and walked the short distance through the town.

Folks greeted her and nodded. Children skipped along beside her. Even dogs accompanied her along the newly paved street.

She let herself in and softly closed the door, announcing, without voice, to the world outside that she was not to be disturbed.

It was the first time she had been to the office since Samuel had lain there on the cot, and it was not easy for her to enter now. But she breathed a prayer, gathered her courage, and went on with the task at hand.

The ledgers were much as she would have expected. Samuel had done well with his practice. There were a number of accounts where instead of indicating "Paid" the word was "Cancelled" instead. Cassandra was not surprised. There were a few outstanding debts, but not many. Most people in the town were conscientious and paid as soon as they could. Cassandra could see nothing of concern with the accounts, and she tucked away the ledger and rose to leave the office.

It was then that she noticed the dust. Samuel had always been quite meticulous. She knew that he would not want a young doctor to see his office so untended. She went to the cupboard where the supplies were kept and began to do some cleaning. By the time she was finished the floors were clean, the furniture dusted, the windows shining again. She was pleased with herself, even though she felt tired, and she wondered why she hadn't thought of tidying it up earlier.

She made arrangements by phone to meet the young doctor at the office the following Monday and he came as promised.

A small man, with glasses, dark eyes and dark hair, Cassandra could see that he was Oriental but that did not surprise her. His letter had been signed "James Otikama."

They went through the office, the books, the supply cupboards, and the young man seemed favorably impressed with what he saw.

"I agree to your offer," he informed her and Cassandra was pleased.

As she walked home alone she felt a measure of satisfaction. She was sure that Samuel would have liked his office to be used—the people of the town to have medical care again. For the first time in many months, and for some strange reason she couldn't explain, she felt that she was alive again.

————

Cassandra found that she slowly adjusted to the years without Samuel—though she never got over her loneliness. She just accepted it as a fact of life. In spite of the number of friends she had—in spite of the love and attention of family—there was no one—ever—who could take Samuel's place. That spot—that special spot that he had built for himself in her heart and life—would forever go unfilled.

And then Virginia also left when Morris sold the drugstore to his junior partner and moved to the city. Cassandra knew that it was the right thing for them to do. Most of their family lived there. But it was still hard to see them go.

"Why don't you come?" coaxed Virginia. "There is really no reason for you to stay on here."

But Cassandra was still reluctant.

This is home, she wished to say. *This is where Samuel is.*

But she just hugged Virginia and said, "Perhaps someday. I'm not ready yet."

A few more years ticked by. Children still came to see

her, bringing their scratches, bruises and pets. They still called her Mrs. Doc when they met her in the street. They still swung on her swing and played in her sandbox. They still ate her sugar cookies and drank cool milk on her back porch.

But the years were taking their toll. Her step was slower than it had been. There were times when she had to stop and lean against something for support if she moved too quickly. For some strange reason, the world seemed to spin around her at such times.

She tried not to let it show, but she knew her own kids had caught her on occasion. They came home often—to check on her, she knew. And each time they came, they had the same mission. To get her to leave the small town, her home of many years, and go to the city where they could take care of her.

She loved them for their concern. At the same time she felt agitated. Life was strange. You started out being told what to do, gained through trial and error, finally earning a chance to be on your own, and then life turned around and took it all away from you and put you right back into the same position from which you had started. Only now it was children rather than parents who tried to tell her what was best for her.

The day finally came when she knew she could hold out no longer.

"All right," she had conceded reluctantly, "I'll go. I'll go this fall—right after I take in the garden."

They exchanged glances over her head, but she was aware of them. She knew their eyes were telling one another that she no longer had any business planting a garden—or taking it in. Why, she could barely get up and down anymore. What if something happened and she couldn't struggle back up onto her feet?

She disregarded the knowing looks and repeated her promise. "Right after the garden is cared for. I'll let you find me an apartment and I'll put the house up for sale."

They had gone away triumphant—and she had retired to her bedroom to weep.

———

Life is so strange, she thought one day as she sat in the living room having her daily Bible study. She had just read the account of the angel of God changing Sarai's name to Sarah and it prompted some thoughts of her own.

"I feel like I've had a name change, too," she said aloud. It didn't hurt her to talk to herself a bit—as long as she didn't get caught. "Oh, not just one. Many," she went on. "Changes all along—with the changes of my life. First I was Cassie Winston. I guess I didn't realize it at the time, but life was pretty easy—quite plush. I was a spoiled, wealthy child—and didn't even know it. Then my name changed to Cassie Smith—and that certainly was a major change. The little girl was no longer. I had to grow up and become a woman—at least outwardly. I wanted to grow up—because I had fallen in love with Samuel.

"But he called me Red. It's funny. If anyone else had dared to call me by that name, I would have been furious. But he called me Red and it—it felt—personal. Like I belonged to him. Me with my horrid red hair. He said it as though—as though he liked it. And that made the color easier for me to endure, too.

"But when he introduced me to others he always said, 'This is my wife, Cassandra Smith. Not 'Mrs. Smith'—but Cassandra Smith. It was as though he was allowing me to be a person. Giving me a right to stand apart from him—just a little bit.

"But even as his young wife—I was still a child in many ways. So selfish. So immature. It wasn't until I met Virginia and wanted what I saw in her life that I decided I really wanted to grow up. Virginia did that for me. Virginia and God. I finally became Cassandra in my own thinking—not little Cassie anymore.

"And then I became Mrs. Doc. It was strange. Just the slip of a little boy's tongue—but it was a new identity. I think Samuel was proud of it. Proud that the people would come to me. Proud that I could help him in the office. Proud that I was able to learn. He was so anxious—so patient about teaching me. He—he enjoyed me working with him. I often wondered if he didn't feel that it was his way of paying Papa back for taking him under his wing. To have a daughter in medicine—as much in medicine as he could allow." Cassandra paused to gaze out the window.

"And now—now I'm leaving. Going off to the city. There won't be a soul there who'll call me Mrs. Doc. I will likely never hear the name again. To the kids I'm 'Mama' or 'Grandma.' To my new acquaintances I'll be simply Mrs. Smith—or Widow Smith. Oh, I hope they don't call me that. I don't think I could stand it.

"But certainly I won't be Mrs. Doc anymore. I won't even be Cassandra."

And she closed her Bible and wiped at a tear.

Then she straightened her shoulders and lifted the once-stubborn chin.

"Well, no matter," she said firmly. "God knows my real name. He always has—always will. He calls me 'My child.' 'Child, I am with you.' 'Child, I will never forsake you.' 'Child, there are no changes in life that we can't handle.' "

———

The porch rocker eased to a stop. The elderly woman sighed deeply and slowly pulled herself to her feet. She reached to the small side table by the chair and lifted her teacup. It was time to get on with life.

The two tall boys were disappearing at the far end of the concrete sidewalk. Soon they would be young men. So many of Samuel's babies had grown to adulthood. Many of them had babies of their own—and some even had grandchildren.

She smiled at the thought of it. Why, he had tended most of the people of the community.

But now Dr. Otikama was caring for the needs of the folk, and he would not be asking for her help at the office. Not that she could have given it. She was too old—too stiff—and she was tired.

She straightened her shoulders and reached to tuck a strand of straying white hair neatly beneath her hairnet. She must get on with her packing. There was so much to do and if she didn't get it done herself, the children would take over and she wouldn't get to sort through the things as she intended.

She let her glance slide over the town that had grown with the years. The new school building that stood proudly on her right—the old, yet new, main street where Morris's old drugstore had been torn down to give way to a more modern building—the grove of planted poplars that marked the borders of the cemetery where Samuel rested. The tears formed and she picked up the edge of her apron and wiped them as they slid down her wrinkled cheeks.

Then her head lifted, her chin thrust slightly forward. It was time to move on.

"Samuel would say, 'Where's your spunk, Red?' " she told herself. " 'Life still holds out a hand to you. Take it.' "

She moved to the edge of the porch and leaned over the railing to pour the remains of the cold tea on the rose bush below. Then she straightened and looked toward the heavens.

"Father," she whispered, "help me with this big change too. Perhaps the last until I make the final one. I'm really going to need you—again."

Her eyes rose to the tall green spires that framed the cemetery, and she managed the faintest of smiles.

"I'll be back," she whispered to Samuel. "It won't be long till my time comes and I'll be back. I made them promise. I told them I wouldn't go unless they brought me back."

She stood for several moments looking out from the front porch while her eyes again scanned the town. No tears came. She was done with weeping. The afternoon breeze teased the silvery hair that escaped her hairnet. Her shoulders sagged slightly, her brow puckered in thought.

And then the green eyes began to sparkle. She pulled

back her shoulders, swished her skirts with a calloused hand, straightened to her fullest height and lifted her head in determination.

"I'll have family there," she reminded herself. "And Virginia will be near. I miss Virginia. Almost as much as I miss Samuel. It will be good to be able to visit with her again." She stopped for a moment and then went on. "And God has never let me down. He will keep His promises to be with me now."

She moved toward the room where the packing boxes awaited her. Her face looked calm—serene. She spoke to herself once more, "Who knows—I might even learn to like it in the city."

The telephone on the hall wall began to jangle. Cassandra went to answer it, hoping that it wouldn't bring bad news.

It was Christina who answered her "hello." She sounded excited.

"Mama? Guess what? You'd never guess. We are moving. George and I. He had the choice of three different churches. He picked Jaret. We're coming there, Mama. At the end of the month."

The flowing words poured out too fast for Cassandra. She couldn't keep up—couldn't sort out the information she was receiving. But one little message did make it through. Christina was moving to Jaret.

And just as I am moving out, she thought. *What a shame!*

But Christina bubbled on. "This is the last pastorate that George plans to take. He thinks that Jaret is a great little spot to retire. We'll just stay on there, Mama."

Cassandra was still busy sorting.

"Mama? Are you there?"

"Yes," managed Cassandra. "Yes, I'm here." Had Christina forgotten that her mother was moving out? That the house was soon to be sold?

"Mama?" A pause. "You won't have to pack."

What was she saying?

"I'll be there. I'll be able to look after you. If you like—that is—if you'd rather stay in your own house, you can. As long as I'm there the others won't mind."

Silence.

"Mama?"

But Cassandra was weeping gently, her heart crying out a thank you to her God. The truth of the call was gradually reaching her understanding. Christina was coming. Christina would be her shield against further change. She would not have to move. She could stay in her own house, in her own town, near Samuel.

"Mama?"

"I hear you," managed Cassandra. "I heard every word."

Then a big smile lighted her face. "I'm glad I'm so slow," she said to her daughter. "I hardly have anything to unpack."